BLACK MONEY

BLACK MONEY

A Novel of Modern Africa

GEORGE H. ROSEN

Scarborough House/*Publishers*
Chelsea, Michigan

Scarborough House/*Publishers*
Chelsea, MI 48118

FIRST PUBLISHED IN 1990

Copyright © 1990 by George H. Rosen.
All rights reserved.
Printed in the United States of America.

Text design by Debra J. Donadio

Library of Congress Cataloging-in-Publication Data

Rosen, George H., 1946-
   Black money.

   I. Title.
PS3568.07649B5   1990   813'.54   86-43196
ISBN 0-8128-3140-3

For Barbara

AUTHOR'S NOTE

Kenya is a real country, but the town of Kigeli, and the Kigeli people, are imaginary. This book is a work of fiction, and details of geography and governmental structure have been changed or invented to fit the purposes of the narrative. All the characters, their deeds and misdeeds, are products of the author's imagination. They are in no way based on anyone, living or dead, who has lived or worked in Kenya or served in that country's government. They have been created to tell a story.

BLACK MONEY

EAST AFRICA, 1970

CHAPTER I

GRIMES LIKED TO spend money. He considered it a small failing, but it added up to six thousand dollars, plus interest, that he owed Bimji. That was forty-three, perhaps forty-five thousand shillings, depending on the rate. But Bimji would want it in dollars.

Grimes liked to drink. There was an army colonel in Northern Province that Bimji paid off to get duty-free liquor to sell to Grimes. The general staff in Nairobi knew it was a hardship to sit up in the desert for a year with the flies and the camel corps and the rotting open-air squash court that the British had left at the post. The garrison guarded the lake, and there was nothing in the lake but freaks—half-dead crocodiles, tilapia fish the size of leopards, and an occasional boatful of archaeologists dredging the bottom in search of ancestral molars. So the army gave liquor privileges to the entire post. Every month a truckload of Johnnie Walker Black Label and Beefeater's came rumbling down the *wadi*. The soldiers drank what they could, and the rest they sold to Bimji who carted it back down to the green country and, in his turn, sold a lot of it to Grimes.

Grimes had plans to sell it to everyone he knew, but they—like many of Grimes's plans—fell through. The cases lived in his back room covered with a tarp so the schoolboys couldn't see that their history master was trying to set himself up as a freelance bootlegger.

Grimes liked to eat. Bimji sold him food, anything he wanted. Frozen legs of lamb came upcountry in Bimji's Land Rover. Meat that came from lambs that looked like lambs. The local sheep and goats were interchangeable, scrawny, infested creatures. The sheep tails went up, and the goat tails went down; that was the only way

13

to tell the difference. But Bimji could get meat from somewhere where sheep were still thick and woolly and ate real grass. And he could get steaks and plump chickens, turkey at Thanksgiving, ham at Christmas. Somewhere he got kosher pickles and Calamata olives, raspberry jam and hand-cut pasta, Swiss candies with cognac centers, and, most miraculous of all in a land where elephants came down from the forests at night, blueberry cheesecake.

Grimes liked to gamble, too. He played poker with Harry Mobley and the other Americans from the agricultural college until they decided it would be charitable to stop. And he played Kigeli games with the old men in a haze of sugar beer. They involved a polished board with small hollows, a pile of black-and-white pebbles, fast hands, instant calculations. He always lost.

Ever since he'd come to the country he'd gone down to the Nairobi casino on weekends. He had bought a dinner jacket and a scarlet cummerbund and had begun to smoke oval cigarettes. Watching the Bluebell Girls he had learned to play baccarat and punta y banco. Badly. He had relied on Bimji to pay his debts.

It was no way for a missionary to behave. Even a half-assed missionary like Jonathan Grimes. Of course—as he often sought to explain—Grimes was not a missionary but a contracted history instructor whom the Methodists in Evanston sent out, not because of any zeal, but because they knew he wanted to go to Africa and was a good teacher. Grimes knew he was a good teacher, too. He just hadn't known what would happen to him given a little loneliness and a little freedom. Not that there was anything that terrible in being six thousand dollars in hock to the local Indian shopowner. Except that Bimji seemed to want his money now. Grimes's work permit and visa were up for review, and if Bimji decided to dun him through the courts it wouldn't look good. Not after he was already in trouble because of Moguru.

Grimes hadn't hit Moguru because he liked fighting. He wasn't quite sure why he had hit Moguru. Except that they were both flying on sugar beer, drinking it from old Coca-Cola bottles in the tin-roofed shack Bimji ran as a bar for the locals. But Grimes hadn't hit Moguru in the tin-roofed shack. He'd hit him in the Sixpenny Cock—the paneled bar of the hotel that Bimji ran for tourists who came through Kigeli on their way to the game park. Grimes didn't know how they had gotten from the shack to the Sixpenny any more than he knew why he had thrown the punch that broke Moguru's jaw.

Or maybe the African didn't break his jaw on the punch. Maybe

14

he broke it on the bar's brass footrail or the Malay spittoon or any of the other colonial relics with which Bimji decorated the barroom. Moguru was a heavy man. Any way you tipped him something was bound to shatter.

The wire in his jawbone was restricting Moguru's own explanation—at least for a few weeks. It hadn't prevented him from signing a police complaint, and it wasn't stopping Moguru from teaching his Swahili and Religious Knowledge classes at the school. He wrote out the notes on the blackboard as he always had, and the students copied down every word.

Grimes had the opposite problem. He wasn't writing anything. His right arm still in a sling from the punch, he droned out his lectures to students who barely spoke up in the best of circumstances but who were now terrified into absolute silence by "the man who broke Moguru's jaw." It was becoming one word in Kigeli.

Grimes had thought it best to offer to pay Moguru's doctor bills. Bimji had been more than willing to lend him the money. Now Bimji was calling in his notes.

"My expenses are rising, Jonathan." Bimji dealt with Europeans in the hotel office, just behind the Sixpenny Cock. It was midday, the sun seeping around the linen curtains. The bar was empty except for old Landers, a former great white hunter for whom Bimji unaccountably kept a hopeless tab. The Englishman was already drunk, asleep on his stool, flies buzzing above his shaggy silver head. "My children, you know, are in school. Foreign schools, very costly. Every few months there is a new tuition bill. So many pounds, so many dollars. You will want tea?"

Grimes nodded. He might as well have tea. Bimji made terrific tea. It was mostly fresh milk, honey, and a smell of crushed spice. Just enough tannin to ground it in reality. Bimji clapped his hands, and a beautiful ten-year-old girl—dark eyes and a ponytail nearly as long as she was—stepped in with a shining brass tray and a china pot.

"The cost of stock for the shop is rising. Bread, groceries, cloth, petrol. Government licenses as well. Everything is licensed now. A day past due and they will put an Indian man in jail, no excuses. You are comfortable, Jonathan?"

Grimes was receiving the lecture sitting on a huge hassock covered with leopard skin. He wondered where Bimji had picked it up.

"I am not a citizen, Jonathan. This makes everything more difficult. In addition to the license fees there are the bribes. There are

15

threats. A single mistake, they say, and they will send me away. Where? To India? To Britain? These are not my places."

The fat man stood erect. The thick, deep folds of his eyelids blinked once, then again. "This is my place. Kigeli is my place."

"Why didn't you take out citizenship at Independence?"

"A foolish error. They gave us the choice of the British or the Kenyan passport. I am a cautious man. I could not know what the new government would be like. I took the British document. Unfortunately, I am an old, cautious man." For an instant Bimji seemed to dream. He swiveled his bulk toward the sunny window. The light pooled on the red, polished floor. It lapped at the Indian's feet but left his face in darkness.

"I intend to pay you, Bimji. I will pay what I owe."

"No doubt. But not now?"

"Not now. I don't have it."

"In that case there is something else you can do for me."

Bimji fumbled through the clutter of his writing desk, a world of thick cardboard files, black ring binders, and school exercise books that he used for accounts—a tiny boy and girl sketched on the cover, holding hands and gazing at a rainbow. He took a lead key on a thin chain from around his neck and opened the desk's single drawer. Then he removed a small leather pouch from within the darkness. The leather looked ancient, worn, soft as skin.

"This was my father's wallet, Jonathan. The British brought him here from India to work on the railroad from Kampala to the sea. He and his two brothers came to Africa. One was killed by a lion while working on the track. The other died of a blood fever. Like myself, my father was also a cautious man. He survived and opened a shop. In this, he kept his money."

He threw the pouch on the table, then pulled a long dark ribbon from a pocket on the wallet's back. "Men were fearful then. The wallet ties around the waist. It is worn underneath the clothes." Bimji walked to the hassock and ran a soft finger along the American's ribs. "On a thin man like yourself—on a white man—it would pass undetected." Bimji patted his stomach lightly. "On an old and fat man like myself, Jonathan—on an Asian man—it would be more visible.

"Take this pouch to the place I tell you, and you will have no need to pay the money you owe me. I will forgive all debts."

Grimes's head hurt, a hangover, he supposed. He picked up the wallet, pulled apart the sides of water-stained leather, and ran a finger—from the hand that was still working—down the center.

"There's nothing in it," he said.

"There will be."

"What?"

"Some checks, banknotes. Some foreign currency."

"Why don't you take it yourself?"

"It is not all what the government might consider legitimate."

"Black money?"

"Let us say 'gray,' Jonathan."

The pain in Grimes's temples began to spread.

"You want me to carry illegal money for you. Out of the country?"

Bimji nodded.

"How much?"

"Since you ask. Fifty thousand dollars."

Bimji picked a playing card box from the table and sat back in a wicker rocker. He opened the box, took out six feathered darts, and swung around to face a board of rotting cork that nestled in the wall opposite the window. "These are very high quality. Not like the plastic ones I leave out there in the public bar. Do you play, Jonathan?"

"Not left-handed I don't."

The fat man smiled at the sling on Grimes's arm. "Ah, the unfortunate incident. Terrible business. I had forgotten."

Bimji whistled a dart toward the board. It missed, completely.

"I consider this money an inheritance, Jonathan. I have worked for it. I cannot pay attention to the technicalities of this or that government office." The dart hit the board this time. Seventeen. "For my children. I must protect it. They are out of the country. The money should be out of the country. If an Asian travels about, there are questions. But a European, Jonathan, a teacher. No difficulties."

A nineteen. Double.

"I could get busted for ten years, Bimji."

"Busted?" Bimji stopped his dart before release. His jowls fluttered.

"Arrested. Locked up. Sent away. Thrown in jail. Imprisoned."

"Ah, yes. Don't worry about it. Merely a small risk." The dart caught a twenty. Triple. Bimji smiled. He never chewed betel. He had perfect teeth. "You know this is fun, Jonathan, to play against oneself. You always win, and you always lose."

"I'm not going to do it. You can sue me." Grimes's whole body was ringing now. Not just the headache, but his sprained wrist and his mashed knuckles. His wounded arm felt as if there were a rainstorm coming.

Bimji put down his darts and patted a drop of sweat from his brow in a slow, elaborate gesture. The owl eyes looked straight at Grimes. "Please get up for a moment. Take this key"—he fumbled in the small pocket sewn into the seam of his silk *kurta*—"and go to the kitchen. There is a small room for storage there. This key will unlock the door. Against the back wall there is a freezer chest. Open it."

The Indian raised his handkerchief to his brow again. "Do not mind the air. In this heat, you know, such a small room. It is rather close."

Grimes took the key and left Bimji getting up to retrieve his darts. He stepped through a sun-dappled passageway into the kitchen where the little girl with the dark eyes was stirring something fragrant in a giant *karhai*. It was all goddamn ridiculous, he thought. If Bimji wanted his money, he'd get him the money from somewhere or other, but he wasn't going to risk his neck.

The girl dashed some turmeric on her palm, sifted it softly between her fingers, then tossed the spice on the bubbling oil. A burst of sweetness filled the air. The girl smiled at Grimes and touched her hands together in the Indian greeting, the stain of the yellow spice coating the tips of her fingers.

"Namaste," the girl said.

"Namaste," Grimes repeated, the storeroom key caught between his fingers. He noticed two closed doors off the kitchen, both covered with a dying paint, one yellow and one white. "The freezer?" Grimes said.

The girl shook her head.

"The freezer. Cold. Cold meat." Grimes rubbed his arms and chattered his teeth.

The little girl giggled, began chattering her own teeth, pointed toward the door on the left, then returned to brewing her spices.

Grimes opened the lock.

The room was small and dark. It smelled of mildew and a more biting odor Grimes remembered but couldn't place. He fumbled on the wall for a light switch. The wall was furry. Short, trimmed fur. Grimes leaned over and ran his good hand along the floor. The floor was furry.

Then he placed the smell. Tanning fluid. He swung his hand

above his head, caught a light switch, and pulled. The room was piled with skins—leopard, lion, cheetah; the white plumes of colobus monkeys; whole, polished crocodile skins; the hides of kob, zebra, Thomson's gazelle. There were bins of snakeskins in the corners and a pile of hollow, burnished turtle shells of the kind the desert tribes used for cattle bells.

Grimes had to grant it to Bimji: he was the soul of diversity. Poaching on top of everything else. He probably had elephant tusks out back. All the more reason not to go ferrying his money around.

A complete lion skin with a stuffed head hung on the wall, its black mane and golden hide catching beads of moisture in the room's dampness. Its eye sockets were hollow, black holes. Grimes rubbed his hand behind the lifeless ears for a moment, then stopped. I must be crazy, he mumbled to himself and walked to the freezer against the back wall. It was an ancient Frigidaire with a cement mixer's roar. On the side was a crude painting of the kind Grimes had seen in country bars; a Masai warrior spearing a lion through the chest, three garish drops of blood, as big as ostrich eggs, spilling from the wound.

Grimes pressed the latch and strained to lift the heavy top.

In the chest were one frozen ham, two trussed chickens, and a schoolteacher in a blue serge churchgoing suit, the wire brace still tied around and through his jaw: Isaac Moguru, his eyes dead as glass.

CHAPTER II

AMONG HIS FELLOW workers at the CID in Nairobi, Inspector Jacob Okiri had a bad reputation. They considered him stuffy, haughty, bullying, condescending, and—in the more distasteful sense of the word—clever. He came from the lake country instead of one of the highland tribes, and he seemed to spend an inordinate amount of time reading foreign newspapers.

Sometimes he read even more peculiar things: bank statements, checkbook records, stock market prospectuses from New York and London—ripping them up into little rectangles and stuffing them into file folders. He had a policeman in Mombasa who regularly sent him up bills of lading from the docks. He seemed interested in the weight of lorries going upcountry and their weight coming back down. Okiri loved license applications: radio licenses, construction permits, firearms control. He had friends in all the appropriate bureaus, and he read the forms and ripped them and stuffed them into the files with everything else.

Crimes of the ordinary kind didn't seem to concern him. They would find five corpses in five days at the end of Mboya Road, all with their throats slashed and their pockets empty, and he wasn't interested. A *panga* gang would terrorize farms in Karen, beheading watchmen and raping nursemaids. Okiri couldn't be bothered.

His personal habits were impeccably dismal. He did not smoke and seldom drank. He chewed gum, a failing he had picked up playing basketball with minor officials from the American embassy. The gum would catch in the gap between his front teeth, a remnant of his tribal upbringing, and he would poke it back onto his tongue with a toothpick and continue his reading, ripping, and filing. In Swahili, they called him *mkaratasi*—the paper man.

What he did do, Okiri kept to himself. His superiors kept little track of him. Half the time they couldn't understand the crimes he claimed he was investigating. His informants were lawyers or accountants as often as pimps and cutthroats. Sometimes they seemed to be both accountants and cutthroats—hard-faced men with Savile Row suits and nervous hands who came into the office saying they would only talk to Okiri and then disappeared with him to the Norfolk Bar.

Today the inspector seemed particularly interested in gasoline and the Starshine Club. On his desk were a stack of tanker delivery vouchers from Total and Esso to the Kigeli-Embu Road Project, five 8 x 10 autographed glossies of Ron Richards and the Jamhuri Bebop Band, currently playing at the Starshine Club, a class photo of last year's Form IV at Bambani Harambee Secondary School, and a magnifying glass.

Okiri ran his eye back and forth between the photographs and circled the Bambani schoolboy, third row, second from the right.

"It is he," he announced.

Inspectors Warumbi and Evans were playing cribbage on top of a computer printout of district cattle theft reports. They did not respond. Neither did Julius Odhiambo who was attempting to telephone the three widows of a charcoal vendor who had been found wrapped in a sheepskin, dead on the Nairobi-Naivasha Road. Kari-uki, the chief inspector, was discussing with a Tsavo game warden the case of an elderly bull elephant killed by the night train from Mombasa. He told Okiri to be quiet.

Okiri stuffed his magnifying glass, the photos, and the tanker vouchers into a folder, tucked it under his long, thin arm, and walked to the door. "I will be at the Starshine Club," he proclaimed, "if I am needed."

Inspector Warumbi told him to save the last dance for Inspector Evans. Inspector Okiri chose not to dignify the remark with a reply. He slammed the door and began to sweat. It was a phenomenally hot day. The bougainvilleas down the median strip of the circuit road were wilting. The highland sky was clear, though Nairobi's growing ball of smog was dense enough to mask the line of the Ngong Hills off to the southwest of the city.

For once in his life Okiri envied the short pants of the uniformed police. He had spent two years of extra study to avoid wearing them. They reminded him of school uniforms, and Okiri had hated being a schoolboy. He had been preposterously tall and thin from the first day he walked off his father's *shamba* to go to the primary school. Until the age of fifteen he had been an athletic incompetent; the school pants never fit, and his classmates held interminable discussions about whether Okiri's legs more resembled dead thorn-tree limbs or stripped sugar cane, pressed of its juice. He had sworn as a teenager—still banging his head on low doorways and paying tailors a fifteen percent premium on his trousers—that someday he would be able to do something memorable to those who scoffed and snickered. While throwing them in jail had not been one of the possibilities he had considered at first, over time it became attractive. In his police career he had only once actually sent a classmate to prison, a local distributor who had been watering Tusker—the "nationbuilder's beer"—to the point of counterrevolution. But, through days of detail, Okiri's spirit was buoyed by the prospect that the Standard VII class at the Elgamet Primary School was collectively, conspiratorially, and unequivocally responsible for every bank fraud and blackmail in the Republic. That faith kept Okiri warm, even on a grimy, searing Saturday like today.

The Starshine Club on Gulzar Street had been a *godown* for a kapok merchant until the kapok market died. It had become a nightclub through the virtues of painted lines. A red circle in the center was the dance floor; a black rectangle toward the back, the stage. The only entity in the place that was not an abstract concept was the bar, about three hundred pounds of bamboo and parrot feathers, designed by someone in London with a Polynesian view of the tropics, and shipped out whole to Africa. The spigots on the beer kegs were a series of Saint Bernard heads in silver plate, auctioned off by the trustees of a cricket club that packed its wickets at Independence.

Ron Richards of the Jamhuri Bebop Band was trying to work the dogs' heads when Inspector Okiri found him.

"A Fender?" the inspector asked. He ran his forefinger over the concavity of Richards's guitar.

"Yes, a first-class American instrument." Richards was a small, brown man. He had a flat nose and two ritual scar marks on his cheeks that gave a permanent, enforced smile to his face.

The inspector leaned over to fiddle with the Saint Bernards. "Jim Reeves used a Martin, didn't he?"

Richards pulled the instrument protectively to his side.

"This is a bass guitar, man. Electrified bass guitar. That is a whole different matter."

23

"I'm sorry, Mr. Muriuki, I am ignorant."

"You could listen to the radio if you want to learn something." His feelings wounded, the musician took a moment before continuing. "How do you know my name?"

"Is Muriuki your name?"

"Sometimes." A faint smile began. "You must be the policeman."

"Come. We will sit down and drink a beer, and you will answer my questions."

The two men walked over to a bare bench against the wall. Inspector Okiri scraped around in his folder and removed a pile of vouchers. "You are the Joshua Muriuki who had a position at the Kigeli Shell-BP petrol station until June of this year?"

"If you say so."

Muriuki was staring up at him with unbelieving eyes as if the inspector's height were some kind of studied deceit. Okiri slumped lower on the bench, but it only pushed his knees up into a new absurdity. His stomach began to bother him.

"Who owns that station?"

"Bimji. Nasty Asian man."

"This is the same Bimji who owns—"

"He owns everything, man. You know that. He owns the station and the store and the hotel and the nightclub up there where I play. That's where I make my reputation, policeman. I don't do anything wrong, just play the guitar." Muriuki gave Okiri that look again. "*Bass* guitar."

"Did the Europeans get their petrol there, the men who build the road?"

The smile on the musician's face became real. "So that is why you're here, policeman? Sure they come there. They are getting the petrol for graders, lorries, all cars. They just drive in and I fill up and Bimji sends them the account. Big account, too, policeman. They don't mind. I write up the gallons, you see. Maybe I put in forty-five gallons. Then Bimji, he tells me to write seventy-five gallons. So I write that. Or Bimji sends in other lorries. I don't know where they are from. They come out of the desert and go back into the desert. I fill them up, too. That goes into the account for the road builders, but you know they're not the road builders' lorries. Bimji tells me to do that. He says the road builders give petrol to the poor."

"To Bimji."

"Right, policeman." Richards leaned to Okiri's ear. "If you killed

24

him for me I could write a song about it. Smash hit song about the tall policeman who shoots the little-boy-fucker."

Muriuki started to strum his Fender. Okiri checked his list. It wasn't there. "Does Bimji fuck little boys?"

"No, policeman. People just say that in Kigeli. He fucks little girls, mostly. Asian girls. He try to fuck Kigeli girls, the old men cut him up into little pieces, slowly by slowly. Then the old women make up the song, they wouldn't need me."

Country people, thought Okiri, distaste in his mind.

"Beside the petrol, was he taking anything else from the road project?"

"I work the pumps, I don't do anything else. Polish the windows, fill the tanks. This is not clean work, you know. It is stinking work." Richards leaned back, reflective. "Someday I go back to Kigeli when I am a big star. I go back then, back to Bimji's station, and I stand there with a cigarette in my hand and a silver lighter in my pocket. And Bimji will be there, and he will be friendly, you know, quite friendly, because I am a big star. He will say, 'Hey, you, Ron Richards of the Jamhuri Bebop Band, I know you when you used to pump petrol, polish the windows. Those good old times, you know. We were big friends, right?' That's what he will say, and he will smile like someone going to photo us for multiracial harmony picture. I will say, 'Sure, man, we big friends.' And I take my cigarette, you know, just like double-oh-seven I throw it right in his face. If I am lucky there is a pool of petrol there, and he goes to the moon. No stops. Then I am a big local hero in Kigeli as well as international music star. Tobacco company gives me a medal, and it is all right with police because Bimji is a well-known very bad man."

Inspector Okiri sipped the warm pilsner. The bubbles calmed his stomach, which Muriuki had now quite definitely upset. There was a time when he would have given the musician a lecture on how—as his training course pamphlet had put it—"the state has a monopoly on justice." But Okiri had stopped giving lectures when he had noticed that the only people who listened were those who made it a rule of thumb always to listen politely to policemen who were six-and-a-half-feet tall. It was Okiri's misfortune that he liked people to listen to him because he was right. As of yet, that hadn't worked out. So he generally kept his mouth shut.

Richards *né* Muriuki swallowed the last of his beer. Four men wearing sombreros were walking in from the sunlight. They all wore patent-leather pointed shoes and had cowboy bandannas around their necks. They stepped toward a row of guitars that leaned against the wall of the stage.

"I am having to play, policeman. If you want any more questions, I think you will ask me now."

Okiri began to stand up, which was for him sometimes a fairly lengthy process. He fretted for an instant about the creases on his trousers, then glanced at his list. "Does Bimji have any European friends," he asked, "any of the engineers from the road-building company? Someone he sees for more than just business?"

Richards shook his head. "The only friend that man has—and he is not much of a friend, I think, he just takes Bimji's money sometimes—that kind of a friend, is a teacher from our secondary school there: Mr. Grimes. He taught me history, you know. I do not just pump petrol up there, policeman. I sat for the certificate examination."

"How did you do?"

"On history, I did very well. Are you going to give Mr. Grimes trouble because of Bimji?"

"Is he a man for trouble?"

"No. He travels a lot, though. He has a woman he sees up near Chuka. Another American. He goes to her only sometimes. I think she is a sister."

Okiri was genuinely shocked. "He is sleeping with this woman who is his sister?"

"Not his blood sister, policeman. A sister in the church."

"A nun? That is no better."

"I do not know. Mostly there they are nuns. Maybe she is a nun. Peace Corps, nuns. She is one of those."

Okiri finished his notes and closed his folder. It was an enormously careful process.

"Why are you so interested in Bimji, policeman?" Muriuki spoke suddenly.

"If a man commits crimes, we are interested."

"But why is the government needing two of you to follow only one crooked man?"

"Two?"

"The little man from the Home Ministry comes here yesterday and asks questions. Then you come here and ask the same questions. Everyone is too interested in coming here. If I am lucky, soon

26

I get a minister or permanent secretary maybe. I think I have my own work to do, not just to answer questions."

"Who was this other man?"

"I told you, policeman. From the Home Ministry. He is not like you. He talks to me in Kigeli, not English, but he is not a Kigeli. He acts like a *mtu mkubwa*—a big man. But really he is no bigger than me. I think maybe you are different, policeman. You are a big man trying to be like a small man, isn't it?"

Muriuki hitched the guitar strap over his shoulder. "You come hear me play tonight, or you go and arrest Bimji?"

"I am not arresting anybody yet." Okiri wanted to get going. He would have to talk with the Home Ministry about this. Tucking the folder under his arm, he moved across the dance floor to the door.

"If you get Bimji, you tell me, OK?"

"I'll do that."

"I think you will be kind to Mr. Grimes, policeman. Greet him for me. Sometimes I think he is a too lonely man." Muriuki put on the sombrero with golden tassels and plugged himself in.

CHAPTER III

"YOU CAN CLOSE it now, Jonathan. He will keep better that way."
Bimji, the darts still in his hand, was standing behind Grimes. The
Asian's breath smelled of cardamom. "Our climate is so hard on
people."

Grimes sealed the freezer top over Moguru's body and followed
Bimji back to his office. The hotel keeper's proposition was straight-
forward. Grimes had one week to pick up and deliver Bimji's money.
If he did not finish the job—or if he chose to discuss the matter
with the police—Isaac Moguru would be found dead in the banana
trees behind Grimes's house, the American's knife in his chest.
"Most regrettable," Bimji said, "but necessary, I am sure, to secure
your complete and open cooperation. Some more tea?"

Grimes shook his head. "No, thank you."

"Whisky perhaps?"

Bimji smiled. Grimes could keep the bottle. Bimji felt himself to
be a generous man. "I recommend you start as soon as possible,
Jonathan. You will get the money at Carr's Hut near Vivienne Falls.
It is twenty miles from here on the road and then six miles up the
mountain. The hut was built by the mountain club but the climbers
prefer the Naaro Moru route to the top now. They are only tourists.
Everyone is in such a hurry. You will spend the night there. At
such an altitude the night sky is lovely. You will have no visitors
except the man I will send to you with the money. He will then
tell you where to deliver it. This is all quite simple, you know. And
very safe. You will enjoy the fresh air."

The Indian climbed on a stool and pulled a framed map of Mt.
Kenya down from the wall. He slipped the paper out from behind

the glass and handed the roll to Grimes. "Here you will start
. . . and here is the hut. Quite simple."

"Five thousand feet up the mountain . . . simple?"

"Quite. But cautious as well. I am eager to avoid chance en-
counters. Don't worry yourself. Please. . . ."

The Asian's whisky had settled Grimes. In the midst of his
resignation, he felt a comforting impulse to practicality. "Do you
have a compass, Bimji?"

"Certainly." The Asian withdrew a ring of keys from his trousers. In the shop, the back case. Take what you need, and leave the
keys with the shopboy. You were a Scout, I presume?"

"A Boy Scout? Why yes, I was. Once."

"Then you will have no problem."

Grimes slipped the map and Bimji's wallet inside his sling. "I
guess that's all I need."

"Then you will go up the mountain soon?"

"Tomorrow, I suppose. In the morning." Grimes looked through
the bar to the outside door. Landers, the old hunter, was gone.
Again, the American felt a puzzling calmness. Having instructions
to follow reassured him, if he were capable of carrying them
through. Right now he didn't know what he was able to do. He
turned toward Bimji. The fat man seemed anxious for him to leave.
"You know, I wasn't a very good Boy Scout," Grimes said. Against
a terrible inertia he pulled himself toward the door and out into
the sunlight.

IN THE MORNING, on the mountainside, there was a mist of faint,
new snow on the treetops. Deep in the forest it dusted the backs
of elephants and puzzled the snouts of leopards settling to sleep.
Twining in the evergreens, mambas sensed the strange cool, and
it sifted over the wings of white-necked ravens nested in the steep,
slant towers of the mountain peak. At the touch of snow, a purple
sunbird left a high rockface. It floated down the wind and settled
on a clump of giant lobelia, probing the rosettes of the swollen
flower for midges to eat.

Grimes wasn't high enough for the snow; on Grimes it was still
raining. He had taken the sling off his arm, though his wrist still
wasn't much good to him, and wrapped the sore limb in an Ace
bandage. For the time being it was fit only to carry Bimji's map
and compass. Not that they did him much good, but in the harsh
drizzle they offered him a reassurance he turned to not so much

when he was lost as when he was frightened—thrown by a gust of wind or the memory of his predicament.

Though he could see the Alpine meadow and bogland that spread out where the forest ended, he was still well below the timberline, climbing a long ridgepath the map indicated would join the main eastern shoulder of the mountain at a point a few hundred feet above Vivienne Falls. The old climbing path was still there, a swathe at times nearly ten feet wide of soft, gold grass that grew between the tall ranks of evergreens. The ground was spongy, giving. A wisp of suction caught each of Grimes's steps, a faint, wearying strain that made the tops of his thighs softly burn with each effort. The path went straight up where it might have cut in switchbacks. It was a road cut by white men who assumed there would always be black backs to carry the tents and cutlery.

As the morning grew, Grimes's steps became smaller, slower. The flesh of his fingers began to swell with the altitude so that the skin flushed and pulled tight over his knuckles. When the morning fog pulled back, he paused to eat at a bend in the trail, spreading out the bottom of his rubber poncho and taking a slice of brown bread and a bag of cashews and raisins from the small pack he carried. Grimes sniffed as he peeled the wax paper back from the stump of bread. The tinned butter must have soured, he thought. The bag of raisins and nuts smelled like shit. Quite specifically like shit: the green, gentle stink of a farm. Grimes dropped the bread on his poncho and walked toward the trees bordering the path. They smelled like shit, too, shit mixed with the dark, carpet odor of wet moss. And the air smelled like a rain forest morning, mixed with shit.

Grimes stepped back from the edge of the trees. The smell was more exact now, coming from a small clearing to the left of the trail, a few yards into the woods. The American pushed through the low brush and squatted in the clearing. At the center of the open space was a pile of steaming excrement, nearly two feet high. The bushes on the side of the clearing opposite Grimes were crushed, trampled, the low branches of the firs snapped and broken.

An old timer, someone like Sid Landers, could sit at the Sixpenny Cock and discourse on the varieties of game excrement, the differences in the pawprints of male and female leopards. If Landers were there, Grimes guessed, he could tell him what the soft, green heap meant, how far away the animal was, how many animals there were. But Grimes was not a hunter. His only communions with the African wild had been filtered through the windshields of rented Volkswagens. Though he had learned to differentiate gazelles by the markings of their back legs—when he had the guidebook with him—he had not learned to distinguish elephant shit from buffalo shit. Or buffalo shit from rhino shit. His wounded wrist ached in the dampness of the forest.

Then the first tree fell down.

It cracked. A strain, then a smash, like the snapping of a mast. The first crack came from below, down the slope away from the clearing. The second was nearer, on Grimes's right, between him and the clearing. It was followed by a bellow—a huge and leathern sound like that of an enormous, leaking bagpipe. It filled every inch of the clearing, seeped into every crevice of bark, every fold of earth, then died. It came a second time—a full, resonant whomp, a bubble of pressure lifting Grimes off his feet then vanishing suddenly, an exploded gas.

Grimes began to piss. He fumbled at his fly, the urine trickling down his leg, until the stream was freed to hit the cool morning air and hiss on the matted grass of the clearing. He stood there holding his prick in his fear-shivered hand while the elephant lurched into the clearing. He saw the beast's legs first, the huge forefeet treading the underbrush, then the trunk and the points of the yellow tusks and the flat, gray forehead snapping the upper branches of the evergreens. The elephant waved his head, cascades of needles sliding down the giant sailing ears, the trunk spinning around the accordion creases of the great gray hide. Grimes could see the immense, heavy gourd of the old bull's penis, feet long, dangling under the giant belly.

Grimes tucked himself back into his pants and retreated a few steps into the trees. The elephant's eyes seemed to follow him, but Grimes couldn't tell if there was any concern in the beast's glance. The creature was agitated. His huge toes pawed at the pile of his own shit. The mash squeezed from underneath, and the beast bellowed again, rearing his trunk. He roared and shuffled around to face the path of trampled bushes that lead from the clearing, his tail swinging in front of Grimes's face, his toes treading the excrement.

It occurred to Grimes that perhaps this wasn't the elephant's own shit.

The elephant was staring down the improvised runway, bellowing again and again, stamping the earth with his feet. The bellows

32

had risen in pitch until they were high squeals, deranged whistles of steam. "Christ," Grimes muttered beneath his breath, and sat down to watch.

At the other end of the runway were two buffalo with thick, scrolled horns. Their eyes had the soft placidity of domestic cattle. But whether from policy or terror they were standing their ground, face front to the elephant, waiting for a charge. The elephant rumbled forward, tusks lowered. In the instant before contact, both buffalo swerved to the side, each scraping twisted horns at the elephant's exposed belly. The animals swiveled and reversed their positions, the two buffalo standing ground between Grimes and the pachyderm.

This time the two buffalo charged with some insane bovine hope that their enemy would break away. He didn't. The elephant lunged right with his head as the buffalo neared him. He took the blow of one buffalo hard against his immobile foot and smashed a tusk through the neck of the second, a giant sear of blood cutting through sinew and muscle. The wounded buffalo knelt in despair, then collapsed. As the elephant pawed his fallen enemy, the first buffalo, dazed but uncut, stood briefly still. His head, which had been lowered in the futile charge, was now raised, pushed back in strangely delicate surprise as if he were a smaller, gentler animal retreating from the touch of an ice cube against its nose. Then the muscles of the huge, dark back shifted, and the buffalo turned tail and ran bellowing down the slope. The bull elephant left the moaning hulk of the dying animal and started to chase the survivor.

Grimes moved. He scrambled back to the pathway, grabbed his pack and ran up the trail, a long, stupid sprint until the breath left him, and the fear, and he felt himself—pants soaked in his own urine, his shirt soaked in sweat—shivering in the mountain air. Don't be a fool, he said to himself, there's a long way to go. He pulled off the pants and shirt, rolled them into a wad, and stuck them in the pack. He was at nearly eleven thousand feet now. The thin air whistled around his naked legs and blew back the hairs on his chest. He wiped himself dry and put on the one change of clothes he had brought, retying Bimji's father's wallet around his waist.

In his crazy run from the animals he had looked only down. Now Grimes could see that he had reached the top of the forest. There were no more trees, only twisted shrubs giving way to meadow grass and monster ferns and flowers, the lobelia that were garden ornaments in the lowlands but here were freaks, eight feet high.

It was a view that held him. Beyond and below him was half a nation, a sweet, broad belt of forest that wrapped the massive mountain, and beyond and below that, stretching forever, the grasslands: mile upon mile of cloud and dust and shrub, infinite against the blue sky. He could see piled clouds coasting in from the Indian Ocean to thin in the heat of the savannah, then mass again on the slopes of the great dead volcano and drift to snow on the sentinel peaks that the British had named for mercenary chiefs, traitors to their own Africa.

Grimes adjusted his pack and checked the compass. The only time he had ever been this high before, Moguru had been with him, he and the dead teacher sharing the lead of a school excursion to the other side of the mountain. A Kikuyu porter had led the way, and the teachers' job was mostly keeping discipline. That was a difficult task near the bottom of the mountain where the boys ran up and down the trail, drifting off from the group to stare or sigh or— illicitly—smoke. It became easier on top, where every step was a leaded effort, and the near-freezing winds, a temperature the students had never known, burned their cheeks and foreheads. The students tossed away the useless souvenirs they had picked up in the forest: improvised bracelets of flowers, staves of green wood, giant mushrooms, and tufts of peculiar rushes that, on the earlier, easier inclines they had waved before them like the cattle switches that as little boys they had used to sway their kinsmen's herds.

Near the mountaintop there had been none of that ease. Two boys had gotten sick with the effort, and Grimes wrapped them in blankets and wiped the vomit from their mouths, nestling them together in the warmest spot by the huge fire of dead brush that their classmates had built in the lee of a looming rockface. When the students were asleep, Moguru and Grimes had stayed by that fire, sipping warm whisky from a flask.

And arguing.

It was amazing to Grimes the amount of argument he could have with a man he basically found agreeable and sensible. Half the time it was about politics, a subject Grimes, with a foreigner's reserve, normally attempted to stay away from. But Moguru galled Grimes. The man thought like a paranoid ward heeler. He dealt with shades of ethnicity that Grimes could barely discern. The Kibara clan was out to control the coffee research station. The Luo policeman was sleeping with the Methodist minister's niece in order to have an informant in the church. The Methodist minister whipped small boys if they came from Mbene. Everyone knew the Catholics only made women from Nkoro nuns. "Why?" Moguru would ask and then answer himself. "Because everyone knows the Nkoro men have shamed the priests who are all weak, landless men from Tendwa."

Then, without preface, like a shift of wind in the night air, they were arguing about death: one of those bizarre disputes about abstractions that seemed to come easily to Africans. Grimes said he thought death came as a shock, that one was never prepared for it. It was like stumbling, being hit by a car. It was always an accident, always an outsider, even in a bed of age.

As far as Grimes could make it out, Moguru thought death could be a kind of character defect, that all deaths were really suicides. Men died of shame, shame for what they had done or thought. The most shameful men invited others to kill them by the shamefulness of their actions. And then he drew back to politics, and his example of a shameful man who invited his own death was Kirera, the opposition leader who had been killed the month before, gunned down before a hundred schoolchildren. A small-time thug looking for a job in the post office had been arrested, tried, and hanged. The whole thing took a week. Moguru said Kirera was a bad man, a man without a heart for the people, and that whether it was the government who killed him or the thug was no matter. Why all the talking, he said. Kirera made his own death from shame, whoever pulled the trigger.

Grimes had thought that a crazy idea and said so, mumbling something about liberal values and the rule of law, then figured it was none of his business and kept on drinking. Which was a good thing because if Moguru could see him now, freezing his ass on a mountaintop to hustle a poacher's money out of the country, he'd probably tell him to go to hell with his rule of law.

Grimes began his walk up the mountain again. Moguru hadn't deserved to die. If Bimji wanted to corral Grimes into being his courier there were less—Grimes searched for a word, the altitude was making him woozy—less *extreme* ways. The Asian must have had his own reason for killing Moguru. It was all so extreme. Grimes was sure he had been right in that first argument. It was an accident. Death was always an accident.

CHAPTER IV

THE HANDLE TO the cabin came off in Grimes's hand. No one had touched the door in years. The wood was swollen, cracked, bathed in the freezing mist from the waterfall that thundered just down the grassy slope. There was a pile of ancient firewood in the corner, brittle like papyrus. Grimes jammed a broom handle up the flue. Clear enough. He piled the wood inside the hearth and threw a match.

The American's boots reeked from the bogland he had crossed above the timberline, a sponge of marsh he'd traversed by hopping from one tuft of swampgrass to another. Half the time he had missed, sinking to his calves through a thin crust of frost and then down into ancient, chilled mud, a prehistoric ooze that stank of age and the thin sterility of high mountain country.

As the fire caught, Grimes toasted his boots and peeled the hardened plaque from his clothes. The sun had set half an hour ago—as always on the Equator, a sudden, disorienting drop. Grimes disliked the way day became night instantly, without preface. He missed the twilights of home.

He scrabbled in his pack for some food. There was nothing to do but wait now. Whomever Bimji had sent with the money wouldn't come too long after sunset unless he knew the route by heart. The moon would not rise for several hours.

Above the mantel was a platform, a cache for dried food. Whatever had been there was long gone. Even the rats who regularly prowled the mountain cabins had deserted the place. There were tiny piles of dust in the corners that, six months, a year ago, might have been droppings. More shit. He had been spending his whole day studying shit.

Grimes grabbed a decaying coffee can, swirled it clean with water from his canteen, then filled it and put it on the hob to boil. The sound of the bubbling water cheered him. It was quite pleasant to be here. To get away. If it all came out right, things would not be so bad. He would have his debt cleared. He could think of leaving Kigeli, traveling some more. After all, Grimes hadn't written the Exchange Control Act, that was no business of his. It was a rotten shame how the government treated some Asians anyway. Criminal. Bimji should get his money; he earned it. Somehow. Poaching, a little chiseling. Nothing so terrible, unless you were crazy about animals. Half of them were probably dead anyway, like that buffalo down the mountain. Survival of the . . . oh, what the hell. It wasn't as if animals didn't kill each other.

But animals didn't stuff each other's bodies in freezers. Maybe they did. The coffee pot began to boil over. Of course they didn't. They didn't need freezers, they ate what they killed on the spot. If animals knew about freezers they would use them. They're just not smart enough. They . . . The flesh on Grimes's fingers holding the pot began to burn.

I had best get a hold on myself, he thought. And he made a glass of powdered milk with the hot water instead of coffee. Powdered milk with brandy from Bimji's stock. It was a sleepy thing to do at that altitude, before a roaring fire. Grimes's eyelids fell. Calming. A mountain wind outside, but it was just like—there was a rustle by his ear—Christmas.

"So you're just the bloody fool I always thought you were."

A nose sniffed at the steaming mug in Grimes's hand, a scarlet nose, broken more than once.

"Brandy is it, Grimes? Don't mind if I do. Not that I drink while working of course. But no work before morning up here, eh?"

Grimes had seen the nose yesterday, snoring at the Sixpenny Cock. Landers, the great white hunter. A black wind from the open door circled the room and fluttered the fire. Landers was tall and soft, a strong man gone to seed. He had coats of fat on the muscles of his arms and a sheriff's potbelly.

"Not that there's much work then. I'll make the delivery, and we'll both toddle down the mountain our separate ways." The old hunter sat on a rotting bentwood chair and ran a mottled hand through his yellow-gray hair. "It wasn't my idea, Grimes. I told him you were useless. That you wouldn't do it. I told him you would just lie there and snivel and be no good at all. But he's smart. He has an eye for personnel. He said that was just why he wanted you. That's what made you perfect. No one would ever think you had the guts for it. The excise men would just wave you on and start questioning the more courageous-looking chaps."

Grimes massaged his aching wrist. "I didn't know you worked for Bimji, Landers."

"Not *for*, lad, *with*. We're partners. Quite even." Landers took Grimes's hand and peeled the fingers back. "How's the wrist?"

"Sore. I don't punch well."

"Keep the fist loose, lad. Otherwise you'll break it every time."

In the back of Grimes's consciousness, the waterfall roared. Again he saw Bimji's freezer.

"You killed him, didn't you?"

Landers grinned and slapped Grimes on the back. "Rhino, lad. Rhino, hippo, eland, lion, of course. Cheetah at a distance, not easy that. Leopard. Elephant, zebra, cape buffalo. Thomson's gazelle, kob. Colobus monkeys in the tree. Giraffe, not at all easy, as you might think. The gait, you understand, is unpredictable, bobbing." Landers locked his eyes on Grimes. "Crocodile. Python. Monitor lizard. Minor reptiles. Not people, lad. Not people. Not even in the Mau-Mau business. They wanted me. Grierby wanted me to scout for the commandos. But I said no. I'm an old man, I can do as I choose, and I went up to Marsabit for four years, shot bull elephant, and let the Mau-Mau and the army and nature take its course. None of my affair, I assure you."

"Then Bimji killed him."

Landers stopped his discourse and peered at Grimes through great watery eyes. "I don't think you want to know this, Grimes. I mean it's not really going to make much difference to you who killed Moguru. I don't think it's good for you to know."

"I suppose you're only thinking of my best interests."

"You don't know anyone killed Moguru. As far as whatever bodies you've seen, Mr. Bimji and myself may just have capitalized on an unfortunate accident."

"An accident involving my kitchen knife."

"Quite possibly."

Grimes realized he wasn't going to get any further with a direct approach. He returned to his brandy and milk while Landers—who did seem to have an authentic talent for wilderness living—began neatly to fry some eggs he had brought up the mountain in his spare bandanna. He somehow produced a pineapple, which he handed to Grimes to carve. They dined quietly but well, the fire sparkling in the hearth, the rush of wind along the moorland outside the window.

"It's the sun that does it, Grimes." Landers sucked at his flask. "Until the age of three or four an African child is just like you or me. But you understand the skull closes more slowly in the African. Like this." The hunter neatly cracked a china teacup as if it were an egg, then pushed the shards back into a near fit. "Until the bones harden the brain is exposed in the gaps, here and here, with only a thin layer of skin for protection. That dulls the brain, stops the growth. Especially at the altitude of the highlands where the air thins out. If the government really wanted to foster education, instead of hiring more of you chaps it could just buy some good, thick hats for the children. Soundest investment they could make, to my mind."

There was no point in arguing with Landers at this stage. Grimes refilled his mug with hot milk and tried to look attentive. The old hunter's nose glowed.

"I gave all my sons fur felt hats. The white blood's probably enough to protect them, but no point taking risks, eh, Grimes?" Landers began to prowl the cabin, the ancient floorboards creaking with the drunken steps. Unasked, he splashed more brandy into Grimes's cup. "Didn't know I had black sons, did you? Legitimate, mind you. I married a Kikuyu in '38 and a Kamba woman after the war. Native ceremonies. I paid the dowries, roasted the appropriate goats. Is that distaste I see on your face, Grimes? You wouldn't actually sleep with an African woman, now would you? You have your delicacy to consider. Oh, a hotel whore in Nairobi every now and then to pull the plug a little. Might be dangerous down there between a native woman's legs. The bush, Grimes, I wager you're afraid of the savage bush. The crocodiles, the jaws. You're a cautious one—you stick to good, clean, white pussy. After all, you are a missionary."

"I'm not a missionary, Landers. I'm a schoolteacher. The Methodists just pay my salary."

"And Bimji pays your bills. Just like he pays mine." The hunter turned and fumbled in the packs he had brought up the trail. Grimes sat frozen in his chair. In his mind he was defending himself. There was something in Landers's ramble that stung him. The women, the bills. Enough truth to make him hurt, to make him want to explain how he had gotten himself into all this.

"Where is your pistol, Grimes?" Landers was holding a rifle to the American's ear. The hunter's drunken breath steamed in front of Grimes's face."

"What pistol? I don't have a pistol."

Landers pushed the cold barrel against Grimes's temple.

"I saw the buffalo down the mountain, lad. I've got the horns over there. You were foolish not to take them. After all the trouble you went to."

"An elephant did that."

"Oh, an elephant did the damage all right. You don't have tusks. But a pistol put it out of its misery, Grimes. A bullet through the brain." The hunter threw a spent cartridge at the American's feet. "Don't be foolish. Don't muck around with guns. Just be a good boy, and carry the money where we say."

Grimes didn't know what to do with his hands. Then he raised them slowly above his head. "I'm telling the truth, Landers. There isn't any gun. You can search me and my things if you like."

Landers did, fumbling through Grimes's pack and pockets. He found nothing, and sat back in his chair across the fireplace from the American, the rifle still across his lap. The flickering fire, his liquor, was pulling the hunter down to sleep. He spoke slowly. "Then there's somebody else on the mountain."

"It could be a climber."

"A climber with a pistol."

"For protection." Grimes was straining.

"It's possible." Landers was tired. Vigilance was getting more difficult.

"Does anyone besides Bimji know we're here?"

The thought seemed to awaken Landers. "Of course not. Unless you told them."

"I don't have any friends that good."

"No, I shouldn't suppose you did."

Ellen's face crossed Grimes's mind for an instant, then faded. Landers kept his hands on the rifle, but a quick drunkard's sleep glazed his eyes. He seemed to Grimes to be willing to wait out the night sitting by the fire.

Grimes was not willing to sit it out. Already his stomach was tight, his mouth dry. He wanted it all to be over.

"Landers, give me the money now."

The older, red-faced man had beads of sweat glistening on his brow. He swatted dully at his hair. The American's words were distant, waking him from a half-formed dream.

"I want Bimji's money and instructions now. I'm going down the trail tonight."

"It's midnight. You're crazy."

"I've got a flashlight and the trail's open. I want to get out of here."

The hunter's drowsy hands began to fumble in his shirt. "Quite silly, I think, Grimes, but . . ." He pulled a soiled envelope from his loosened belt. It fell to his lap.

Grimes cajoled him. His voice was desperate, soothing. "The less time we're together, the better."

The hunter handed Grimes the envelope. Landers suddenly appeared to Grimes to be only what he was—an old man sitting by a fire, his brain drunk, sleep-heavy hands folded over a rifle nestled in the folds of a stomach swollen by too much brandy, too much waiting.

"My wives both died in childbirth, Grimes. My sons are with their families. My share of all this goes to them. So you'd better take care, you bugger." His words flared into vehemence, then sank again.

Grimes shouldered his backpack and switched on the flashlight. He nudged the door open. Wind circled the cabin. The night sky was diamond clear. Brilliant pinwheels of starshine, gem glow of constellations. The path ahead was blessed with light, easy all the way.

INSIDE THE CABIN Landers snorted, his head spilling against the side of the chair. He might as well get to bed, he thought. He unrolled a sleeping bag on the rickety wooden bunk. Grimes was an impatient fool. But there was no real danger going down the trail. The flashlight would be enough to protect him. The big animals didn't fool with humans if they made enough noise, gave them fair warning. He'd never met an animal yet that craved the taste of humans. Too bitter, he supposed, then laughed. He hadn't the faintest idea what a human tasted like. He'd had monkey, a sliver out of curiosity. Salty. Then the repulsion had set in at eating something so close to man, and he had thrown up, much to the amusement of his bearers. Whatever it was like, animals stayed away from it. Grimes would make sufficient noise, out of sheer fear,

42

most likely. God's way of protecting cowards—making them noisy. It was the strong, silent types who stepped on snakes.

The hunter stoked the fire then lay on the bunk. There was no harm in one more. He poured the last of the brandy Grimes had left behind into his canteen, swirled it down with the water. The warmth crawled back into his belly. Bimji wasn't a bad sort. Neither was Grimes. None of them were if they treated one another properly.

Landers closed his eyes. His neck was sore from pulling the pack in the climb. He turned, a heave of weight.

Near sleep he heard a rustle, then a knock at the door. Grimes back, no doubt. "Is that you, lad, afraid of the dark?" The door opened and Landers brushed the sleep from his eyes. Grimes was already too far down the hillside to hear the shots.

CHAPTER V

OKIRI MADE A number of inquiries. He called his tribesman Okello at the Home Ministry. Okello was a clerk-typist with an excellent memory. As far as he knew, no one in the ministry was especially interested in Kigeli or in Asians who were stealing petrol from construction companies.

But while Inspector Okiri puzzled through his paperwork—some lorries licensed to a dead man, the records of a Mombasa curio shop that was exporting inordinate numbers of elephant foot cuspidors— Okello called back. A car had been signed out of the ministry pool the day before, to Section 21, destination Kongoru, a small market town high on the Kigeli side of Mount Kenya—might that be of use? Perhaps they were the ones who had spoken with the singer at the Starshine Club?

Okiri filled out his own auto requisition. Section 21 of the Home Ministry was devoted to what were called "Special Projects" and reported directly to the minister, the Honorable Charles Mathenge. An attorney of some note before he entered government, he was colloquially and rather cautiously known as *kifaru*—"Rhino." His nose, weight, and toughness accounted in equal measure for the nickname. Mathenge offered the operatives of Section 21 his protection and confidence. In return, the "minister's boys," as they were known, offered him strong arms, closed mouths, and absolute devotion.

Section 21 was responsible for investigating crimes against the state. Its men kept an eye on the opposition. They kept an eye on those potentially sympathetic to the opposition. They kept an eye on those who someday might constitute an opposition. They defined the opposition as those whose interests were antagonistic to the

Republic of Kenya, to the Government of Kenya currently in place, and to Charles Mathenge.

It was not wise to attract the interest of Section 21.

A coffee-grower named Abel Kiano had once complained to the police that his fields were being destroyed by the parade of lorries and vans that had been dropping visitors off at Charles Mathenge's *shamba*. The minister had had a lot of visitors that year—men, women, and children with feathers in their hair in the colors of the government party. They came every morning, packed in creaking truckloads, and left in the evening. It was said by some people—people who had attracted the interest of Section 21—that these visitors had come for oathing ceremonies, that they swore in the blood of goats allegiance, not to the nation, but to the minister and to the minister's tribe. It was an oath the breaking of which would bring death.

Of course, as Mathenge pointed out in Parliament, there were no such oaths. The great number of goats that came to his *shamba* were for feasting, not oathing. The visitors were loyal political supporters, many of them relatives. The minister, if he might be permitted to say so himself, was a man of generous temperament and he could not help but share his good fortune and bounty with his friends and relations.

When Ezekiel Kirera, the opposition spokesman whose murderer Section 21 itself later brought to justice, asked the minister how many friends and relations he had entertained, the minister replied frankly that the number was somewhere between 25,000 and 30,000 persons.

Kiano, the next-door neighbor, had not joined the celebrations or oathings, if there were oathings. As he had told the local party worker who had invited him, he had too much work to do with his pineapples and coffee trees. But he was bothered by the tracks through his fields. He put up a wire fence at some expense, but it was knocked over. A week or so after Section 21 began to have its eye on Mr. Kiano, he was struck by one of the trucks carrying Mr. Mathenge's guests. It was quite certainly an accident. The brakes were simply not adequate to hold back the great weight of the merrymakers. The minister sent his condolences. His offer to Kiano's widows to purchase the dead man's *shamba* was gratefully accepted. The driver, an employee of the Home Ministry, was said to be disconsolate.

Inspector Okiri did not know about Kiano's accident. He did know that friends told him to stay away from Section 21 business. Okello, the clerk-typist, told him that. His supervisor, Inspector Kariuki, told him that.

But Okiri was a man rather quick to anger. He considered it one of his principal faults. He disliked other agencies investigating his cases. If Section 21 itself did not think it worth their while to discuss the issue with him, then Okiri would continue to pursue the matter of Mr. Bimji and the petrol on his own. He decided to visit Kigeli.

HE ALMOST MISSED seeing the hitchhiker. The little man waving his arm was practically lost in the shadows. Okiri slowed the Capri and pulled it onto the shoulder. It took a moment for his bones to settle from the jarring of the corrugated road.

The hitchhiker had a fine covering of red clay on his legs. He was wearing torn shorts and a blue undershirt and had a green canvas sack thrown over his shoulder. Okiri beckoned him to come around to the front seat of the car. Okiri spoke no Kigeli—the language of the district. They conversed in a rough Kiswahili.

The man was returning to the town of Kigeli, near where his father had a small *shamba*. He had been up to the mountain forest to gather *samba,* a dark red wood that could be bent easily to human or animal form. He made carvings of lions and giraffes to sell to the tourists at the National Park. Would Okiri like to see some?

The inspector was tired. Otherwise he might have questioned the man about chopping wood in a protected area. As it was, he listened to the small, finely muscled man who kept rummaging in his bag, pulling out chunks of the somber, knotty wood to show the policeman.

The man was really quite muscular. Almost as if he worked with weights. The outdoor life, thought Okiri. The inspector felt a shiver of nostalgia for his own father's farm. Since he had left it as a young boy, except for school vacations when he had generally been treated as returning royalty, he remembered his home mainly as a place where his mother and grandmother competed in cooking for him between their stints of digging in the fields. His principal task had been to watch the three cows—who seemed well able to watch themselves—and to help his mother, and his father's other wives, pick the young tea leaves when the plants had grown to the proper height.

Okiri pulled the Capri around a long curve, and a small waterfall broke through the red cliff and gurgled through a pipe under the

47

roadbed. On the downhill side of the road the land slanted sharply down through a grove of coffee trees to a furious stream.

"This is my clansmen's land. This is where we started." The small man swept his arm over the coffee trees. "Of course now we are everywhere in Kigeli. Quite prosperous."

"You must be good farmers."

The little man smiled. "Good farmers and clever men." For the first time, Okiri noticed he had a scar, a deep scar running along the line of his chin, half-hidden by a meager goatee and the dark, almost purple color of the man's skin.

The road pulled away from the stream and began to climb a ridge. The Capri coughed slightly with the strain. Okiri downshifted, and his eyes momentarily glanced at the floor. Something puzzled him.

"Where did you get your shoes?"

The hitchhiker looked at his feet. "My shoes?"

"They're American basketball shoes. Where did you get them?"

Okiri had seen them in his weekly games at the embassy gym. He had a pair himself. But he had never seen them on a farmer's feet before.

The small man stopped his smile. "From my brother in Nairobi."

"Does he play?"

"Basketball? Why yes, he plays. With the foreigners. Americans, Italians, Russians."

Okiri was surprised. He would have thought of the man as someone who would refer to all whites as *wazungu*—foreigners.

"Perhaps I know him. I play myself."

"I do not think so." The farmer's jaw was clenched.

"But I would. There are not so many of us who play with foreigners."

The little man paused for a second. "His name is Titus Kimani."

Of course he was lying. Okiri could see that in his face. But he couldn't see why. It seemed a completely innocuous matter. Perhaps the shoes were stolen. But that didn't make sense either. Where in Kigeli could someone find a pair of Converse All-Stars to steal, especially ones that fit?

"I don't know him."

"No one knows everyone in Nairobi. A man would be a fool to think that."

"Quite so."

Okiri let the matter drop. As they went along the winding descent

48

to Kigeli town the hitchhiker sat beside him, his face still, staring straight ahead, his hands clutched tight around the canvas sack. The inspector let the man out at a curve just before the road fell to the tarmac of the town. The small man didn't thank him. Okiri ascribed it to the sullen temper of the Kigeli and began to concentrate on Bimji.

He spoke first with an official of the road-building company. Mr. Hans Schneyermann was indeed aware that gasoline use on the project was excessive. But he seemed reluctant to make any accusations. There was a lot of uphill work, he explained, hauling great weights, that would account for more substantial costs than constructing the roadbed in a flatter, more docile country. Schneyermann offered Okiri a bit of thinly sliced ham and a chunk of sweet cheese he said was a specialty of his home, a place called Westphalia. He also pointed out, as no doubt Bimji would, that since the gasoline was stored in Kigeli town where the altitude was lower, the temperatures more extreme—they were after all only a few miles from the Equator—losses from evaporation were great.

Schneyermann offered Okiri another chunk of cheese. The German was a happy man. He liked the sun. He liked the landscape. He liked the way the clouds blew in off the savannah in the morning. He liked ripping slices off the red earth and grading a roadbed straight into the green of the mountain. He liked his work. The only thing he didn't like was the government not allowing him to hunt.

A little graft wasn't going to bother him.

"Do you ever box, Inspector Okiri?"

"No."

"Wrestle?"

"No."

"Only a thought. Your height, of course, made me think." They shook hands at the door. "I miss getting hold of people occasionally here. Back home all we engineers used to wrestle. It is a tradition."

Okiri thought the man a fool, but he liked his food. When he left he took some ham, cheese, and a piece of the dark bread Schneyermann called pumpernickel, all wrapped in wax paper.

At the Kigeli Coffee Cooperative Hotel, the desk clerk was a police informer. Okiri had his name from the locals. The man was a Somali Muslim, teak-colored. He winked constantly. Okiri wasn't sure whether it was a signal or an infirmity. His name was Abdallah and, assuring the inspector he knew everything there was to know about Bimji, he invited Okiri into the kitchen to talk in private.

Abdallah hacked some pieces off a cold, cooked chicken, mixed them with a bowl of warm rice from the stove, and poured himself a glass of milk. He did know everything about Bimji, all of it sixth hand. Okiri learned again that Bimji fucked little Asian boys. They were brought to him in Land Rovers from the countryside in the dead of night and taken away before daybreak. Everyone knew this. A woman that Abdallah knew, whose sister's husband had once worked for Bimji, had heard screams one evening from the back of the hotel. As near as Okiri could figure it from Abdallah's enthusiastic but undisciplined telling, that had been about five years before Independence.

Bimji liked eating pickled fish. Abdallah had seen the empty tins in the garbage dump. Abdallah considered the practice disgusting. Bimji often shortchanged people in his hardware store. He was abusive to servants, scornful of Christians and Muslims, and, like all Asians, was known to chew bits of a peculiar green substance wrapped in silver foil that made his eyes glaze over like those of a lion fresh from a kill.

He was also a well-known criminal, though Abdallah himself had no proof of this. Neither did the husband of the sister of the woman that Abdallah knew, nor, as far as Okiri could see, did anyone Abdallah had ever met.

After the Somali told him that Bimji was known to drink the blood of monkeys—which he kept in the pyramidal containers used for ultra-heat-treated milk—Okiri decided he had another appointment. The information cost the inspector twenty shillings. He therefore felt it was all right to accept a small container of the chicken and rice. It looked quite tasty.

Night had fallen while Okiri was locked into Abdallah's kitchen. The moon hadn't yet risen. Okiri stumbled slightly on the gravel while walking to his car. By day Kigeli had been ugly, a hasty concatenation of houses—cinder block, wood, tin—dipped in the red dust, piled against eroded gullies. But the man-made things faded away at night, and Okiri could see the land now, the mass of the mountain against a forest of stars. He opened the car door, then thought better of it, closed it, and walked down the tarmac to the edge of town. His eyes were getting used to the darkness. After a five-minute walk he came to the end of the pavement.

50

To the left, the road wound off into the trees, but to the right, beyond a steep dark ravine, were the low, squat barracks Okiri knew were the District Prison. He could smell the smoke from the cookfires where the prisoners' families were preparing dinners for the men, then see the haze as it caught the first rays from the rising moon. The prison had the best view in town, endless dark ridges rolling to the dim-lit plains. It was a vision of pure freedom. The only boundaries were unseen: the desert to the north, the ocean, numberless green miles to the east.

This was not the land of Okiri's people. His ancestors had lived far to the west, above Nyanza, the great lake that the Europeans had called Victoria. Okiri could not understand the language of the people who lived here any more than he could speak French or German. But they were of the same nation. They shared this land, Okiri's own people and the Kigeli, even the thieves and pickpockets down in the District Prison.

The inspector stood up from the roadside and swept the dust from his trousers with long, loose arms. He had the night before him. If no one could tell him what he wanted to know about Bimji, then he would have to see for himself. He turned back on the road toward town and the Asian's hotel.

CHAPTER VI

OKIRI SAW BIMJI on the veranda of his hotel. He was sitting outside the bar, drawing quietly on a cigarette. He seemed to be waiting for someone; the darkness and distance hid the policeman from his view. As he was about to step up to the hotel and present himself, Okiri suddenly changed his mind. He skirted the gravel drive, ran quickly across the small, landscaped lawn, and squatted beside a row of bushes that divided the hotel ground from an arm of the forest that reached down from the high ridge behind the hotel.

Okiri patted clean a small sitting space. From here he could see not only the hotel veranda, but—through the side windows—the interior of the bar, the hotel kitchen, and Bimji's office.

The bar was open for business but seemed empty except for the barman, a thin, worried Kigeli who wore an ancient red vest, the velvet of which was torn and spotted like the skin of a diseased housecat. The barman stood idly, rolling the dice that belonged to a shutbox gambling game, until Bimji shouted at him through the porch door and the bartender pushed the game away and officiously began to polish glasses.

Bimji sat still at his wicker table on the porch. He seemed to be looking down the driveway toward town, the low, glimmering lights of his gasoline station hissing a "BP" into the night. The evening air was cool, and in his hiding place Okiri pulled the collar of his coat up around his neck. He felt in the jacket's breast pocket and took out Schneyermann's pumpernickel and ham. No harm in eating. In stealthy, quiet motions Okiri made himself a sandwich. The hotel owner sensed something at the edge of his hearing—the whispering of crickets perhaps—and kept his vigil.

An hour passed. Bimji seemed to check his watch nearly as often

53

as Okiri did; then the Asian blew out the kerosene lantern on his table and retreated inside the building. His face had a harried look as if he were trying to remember something. He dismissed the bartender, who, at Bimji's orders, closed the porch door and swung open the shutters of the front window that kept watch over the driveway. The bartender hung his sad vest on a nail behind the bar and disappeared into the kitchen and out the back door.

Just as Okiri finished the last of the sandwich, Bimji began to sing. He had, oddly, a pleasant voice. First he sang an Indian song, full of dips and shakes, but with a sweet, steady rhythm that made Okiri think of the men of his grandfather's age-group who used to chant long, proud boasts of the old days to the children at night. Then Bimji sang "Your Cheating Heart," a song the American Jim Reeves sang on the radio that was a favorite of the inspector's. He sang it solemnly, slowly, as if the notes were being spooned out of a honey-gourd. The words were sad ones: a man who could not sleep because of the betrayal of his loved one. The sadness lingered for a moment after the song's end, and then the Asian pushed up from his chair and stepped into the kitchen.

There was a closed door that Okiri could just barely see in the back wall of the kitchen. Bimji walked to it, stopped, then started again. Suddenly the Indian looked directly out the side window to the hedge where Okiri was squatting. His eyes swept over it, and Okiri flattened himself along the cool ground as if the man's hooded gaze were a spotlight beam. The inspector's breath stopped, but he was not seen, and Bimji opened the storeroom door.

Okiri could not see into the small room. A minute went by after the hotel owner entered. From his hedge, the inspector heard a click: the opening of a chest. A faint glow came from the storeroom into the kitchen. There was a scraping, the sound of the chest lock clicking again, and Bimji reemerged into the light.

He was carrying a giant turkey drumstick in his hand, shreds of stiff flesh hanging from the leg's thick end. The Indian threw it into a pot of boiling water on the stove, his heavy face smiling at the bubbling like a proud father's.

Outside in the night, Okiri grew hungry again. His joints were sore from the squatting. He sat on the cold ground and stuck his legs out of the hedge, in the direction away from the hotel. While Bimji tended his turkey, the African sorted the leftover chicken and rice from the Coffee Hotel kitchen out of the tin foil. The rice was cold on his tongue, soft starch coating the grains and sticking to the roof of his mouth. If he closed his eyes he could mix the rich odor of Bimji's curry with his own bits of stringy chicken.

The Indian's meal lasted long after Okiri had finished his own. But Bimji no longer seemed as happy as he had been while singing. He checked his watch again and again, between sips of lager. Twice he got up from the kitchen table, walked into the bar, and stared down the long driveway. Worry darkened his face. His hands became nervous, poking at the meat on the turkey bone, throwing bits of rice to the floor where a gaunt orange cat loitered near his feet. Then he deserted the kitchen table, his plate half full, and walked to the bar window, the beer bottle clutched in his hand.

Okiri didn't know what to make of it. The night air and the cold rice were leading him to regret his amateur surveillance. This was not the sort of work he did best. He might have spent the evening with ledgers in the relative comfort of the Coffee Hotel, preparing a list of questions to ask Bimji in the morning. But he had acted on impulse, a twitch of his mind that told him directness would not work here, that Bimji would be as adept at confusing the inspector as he had been at convincing Schneyermann of his geniality or the Somali hotel clerk of his cartoon evil.

But all Okiri could see tonight was a man waiting for something or someone who was not coming.

The inspector was about to settle on believing that Bimji really was expecting a truckload of young boys from the north when he heard a rustle of branches, then a heavy sigh and a loss of breath.

It came from across the hotel lawn, from the hedge parallel to Okiri's own that ran along the opposite side of the veranda. There was a man there: a small man lying on the ground, his head poking from underneath the shrub branches. His eyes did not meet the inspector's. Instead they were staring up toward the veranda. He, too, was watching Bimji.

Okiri recognized the stars on the clean white canvas of the man's shoes and the tight, strong muscles of his arm in the moonlight. The hitchhiker seemed to have fallen or tripped and was waiting for an opportunity to hide again. Silently as he could, the little man withdrew back into the hedge.

Bimji at his table had noticed nothing. Okiri thought he must be half drunk or half asleep. The inspector would see to him later. For now, Okiri turned under his own hedge and began to circle around the back of the hotel to the hitchhiker.

The inspector walked tentatively; his long legs were stiff, unsure of the ground, and he distrusted his own awkwardness. In the years since he had stumbled on primary school football fields, he had gained strength to match his frame, but he knew he had never acquired grace. His feet were born to make noise. Bent over under the shadow of the hedge, he stepped slowly the length of the bushes, then ran across the yard to the eaves of an old stable behind the hotel.

The decaying building was the fantasy of the first British District Commissioner of Kigeli, whose house the hotel had once been. His two bachelor passions had been horses and music. He had brought with him a stallion, a mare, and two geldings, all of them huge, spirited, and white as snow. The horses had been kept in the large stable, now riddled with white ants.

Bimji used the building as a storage shed for his hardware store. A single window looked in on stacks of tin pails and cords of new *pangas,* their blades greased and unsharpened. Okiri had forgotten that he might need a weapon. He had not requisitioned a sidearm for the trip to Kigeli. The bureau required three forms and four days to arm an officer. Okiri stretched his fingers. There was a *jembe* leaning against the stable door. The inspector grabbed the handle of the short hoe and brought it to his side. The blade felt like rough stone, covered with rust.

Under the protection of the stable, Okiri slipped to the far side of the hotel. The hedge that covered the hitchhiker ran flush against the trees of the forest. There would be thirty yards of darkness to cross before he was next to the other watcher. The inspector tightened his grip about the handle of the *jembe.* With his free hand he felt the earth: soft, giving. He had a momentary twinge of the old pain at being too large, too long, and began to scuttle along the ground in the blackness.

The first few steps were fine. Then the fall and the wave of smell were simultaneous. His right foot plunged to the ankle in a mash of eggshells, his left collided with something wet and metallic, and he glided in a hail of tin cans down the slope into the reek of a garbage pit.

There was no hiding the noise. The hitchhiker wheeled around, a glint of gunmetal in his hand. His eyes jittered, like a lizard's scanning the darkness. Okiri pulled his *jembe* from the slime, ready for a last stand, but the small man was not attacking. Okiri saw him glance back at the hotel veranda and then run off into the woods.

56

The inspector stumbled to his feet, every flail sending up a new clatter. Dripping refuse, he made his decision and went crashing off into the forest after the man in basketball shoes.

Bimji heard the riot in the compost heap back behind the hedge. The commotion snapped him out of his lethargic vigil. "Bloody fucker dogs!" he screamed, then yelled it again at the top of his voice.

The Asian smiled. That was good. It seemed to clear the air. He had long ago decided that English was the native language of domestic animals.

He yelled again, a new string of curses he had learned as quartermaster to the King's African Rifles, and the noisy scavengers seemed to heed, clattering off into the bush, too scared to bark. The whole thing woke Bimji up. He got a new bottle of lager from behind the bar and began to sing, happy and refreshed again, waiting for the dead man to come down the mountain and tell him that all had gone smoothly.

CHAPTER VII

TWO ITALIAN PRIESTS who were keen climbers found Landers's body. He had been carried up from the cabin nearly a half mile and dumped on the main path. It was cool enough so that the frost kept him relatively intact and high enough so that the vultures had not yet found him. The priests did what they could in the denominational uncertainty and packed him down the road.

The local police were confused. They called Nairobi to ask what to do with the man with bullet holes in his head and found out—somewhat disconcertingly—that there was already a CID inspector in Kigeli. He was staying in the Coffee Hotel but temporarily out of his room. They brought the corpse to the District Hospital, where it was kept chilled while they tried to locate the relatives.

Grimes had returned to his cottage at the secondary school. He had six days left of the week Bimji had allowed him. He was packing for his trip to the coast when he heard of the hunter's death. Moguru's wife told him. She was a shy woman who had been training to be a primary school teacher, until Moguru made her pregnant and a hasty marriage was arranged. When Moguru was off making one of his trips "to see about his *shamba*"—a remote and totally improbable piece of farmland tucked away in the Nyarene Hills—she took over his classes. Sometimes she would muster the courage to have tea and bananas with the other teachers. As far as she knew, her husband was seeing about his *shamba* now, and she had come to borrow a book from the American teacher.

As they spoke, his private knowledge of her widowhood did something peculiar to Grimes's esophagus. He kept swallowing as she talked and scanned his bookshelf. The news of Landers's death collapsed his breathing altogether. There was a shiver in his lungs, and he coughed and gasped until the woman ran to his kitchen and brought a glass of water. She wanted to help in some other way but could think of nothing that her absent husband would not consider an affront. She sat by Grimes, embarrassed, her hands clutched together, until he was able to talk, then stuffed a volume of *The Prisoner of Zenda* in her purse and excused herself out the door, her mind puzzled by the strange ways Europeans seemed to mourn the death of one of their own.

Grimes traded the water for whisky. He needed some time to settle himself. He tried to trace the steps that led from owing Bimji some money and slugging Moguru in the face, to his current disaster. *His* disaster? That was being a bit egotistical. After all, Moguru and Landers were dead. It was more their disaster. And Grimes hadn't a clue why Bimji had killed them—if Bimji had killed them.

The only possible reason for Bimji to kill Landers—to cover the traces of the transfer of his money—would apply with equal force to Bimji killing Grimes. After he had gone to the coast, of course. After he had delivered the money.

Grimes looked over Bimji's instructions. He was to travel to Malindi and register at a good hotel as if he were taking a holiday. During his second day at the beach resort he would rent a fishing boat for the afternoon and go out to sea a few miles. Offshore there would be a dhow—one of the old Arab sailing craft that were still used as coasting vessels, sometimes going all the way around the Arabian Gulf to India. Grimes was to motor out to the dhow—it would be named *Mzimu*, "The Spirit"—and give the envelope with Bimji's money to the captain. The vessel's captain was a trusted employee of Bimji's brother. He would give Grimes a receipt to be returned to the Indian in Kigeli. And that would be the end of that.

Assuming Bimji let him live.

But Bimji really had no reason to kill him. Suppose that, in a burst of self-righteousness, I try to turn him in, Grimes thought. If I told about the black money I'd be implicating myself. And if I spoke of Moguru's body, what proof would I have? The body would have disappeared by then, and the police would still be likely to assume that I was the one who had a motive. There was no connection between Bimji and Moguru. There was a connection between Grimes and Moguru.

Bimji could also protect himself by pointing out the money Grimes owed him. As he still had a motive for killing Moguru,

Grimes had a motive for defaming Bimji, for making a false accusation.

Grimes rubbed his wrist. He had accumulated felonious motives the way one might collect burrs walking through a field. But he hadn't committed the crimes.

Though he wasn't sure Bimji had either. The feeling he had had climbing up the mountain came back to him. Killing Moguru, killing Landers. It was all so extreme. Bimji was a cautious man, a man who shaved pennies and kept accounts. He was too frightened to carry his own money out of the country. Grimes could not believe he was a killer. But then who was?

He would talk to Bimji before going to the coast. Without the money in his pocket. He would leave that in a safe place. There was nothing wrong with talking. Grimes opened the homemade box in which he kept his letters and papers.

Money.

Grimes tried to keep things in alphabetical order.

Money.

He thought a moment, then thumbed through the dog-eared documents until he came to a packet of probate papers and his letters from the church group that paid his salary. Money. Grimes dropped Bimji's envelope between "Methodists" and "Mother" and caught a ride on the country bus into town.

BIMJI WAS FURIOUS that Grimes had come to see him again. He watched the thin young man hem and haw and twitch his fingers for an eternity until Bimji realized that the idiot thought he, Bimji, had killed Landers. Since he had never even considered the devious reasoning that the American appeared to attribute to him, it was something of a shock. But then it became anger.

"Landers was my partner, Jonathan. I did not kill him. I would not think of killing him. We were colleagues."

"But he was a drunk. He might talk."

"That is right. He was a drunk. But unlike some others of your race, when he was drunk he did not boast or brag, he did not hit people and regret it later. He was able to control himself. Unlike others.

"He was a useful man. He could deal with Europeans in ways that I find difficult. He had useful acquaintances."

"And he was a good shot?"

"What do you mean?"

Grimes's eyes were on a lampshade: zebra. "The hides and skins in your back room. The ivory. Landers was a hunter."

"Such hunting is now illegal."

"But it goes on."

"Yes it does. You are right, Jonathan. Landers was a good shot. That, too, was useful."

The Asian looked nearly as afraid as Grimes felt.

"You must understand I did not kill him. I do not know who killed him."

Grimes tried to believe him. Maybe, he thought, if the Asian were frightened enough, he would stop the whole thing, call it off.

"You realize that whoever killed Landers will probably want to kill you?"

Bimji resisted. "He might have had his own enemies. People not connected with our business together."

"Is that likely?"

The Asian considered for a moment. An aging, drunken white hunter who spent most of his money taking care of the relatives of his African wives and children. No, if there were enemies, Bimji had given them to Landers.

"Maybe you should stop this and keep your money. Why take any more risks?"

"I will get the money out, Jonathan." Bimji crushed the feathers of a dart in his fingers. Then something occurred to him, and the fear that Grimes had seen in his face disappeared. "And I will get myself out." He dropped the mangled dart to the floor and sat down.

"You'll leave Kigeli?" The idea stunned Grimes. He couldn't imagine the place without Bimji's presence. Who would run the hotel, the store, the gas station, the nightclub? Grimes began to see the hold that Bimji had over the life of the town: a penniless exile who had sold, and bought, and saved himself into the gaps, the places the British had not wanted to fill and had not permitted the Africans to fill; a scavenger, a filler of needs.

"My kind of home can be carried about, Jonathan. I have done it before."

"What if I don't help you?"

"You will help me for your own sake. You are aware that if I speak to the police they will have little doubt that you killed Landers."

"I could tell them the truth."

Bimji smiled for the first time since Grimes knocked at the door. "The truth, yes. Do you think Moguru is still in my freezer?"

The fear came back to Grimes, spreading like the warmth of a drink. "You said you wouldn't bring him to my house if I did what you said."

"That is still true, if you cooperate. I am only explaining why you must continue to help me. You must remember that you have now committed two murders. That is very serious, you know." The Indian looked at him with dark eyes. He looked like a man made of ash, incomparably old. "Do not take my desires lightly, Jonathan. You must trust my wishes."

"Two murders?"

"Two murders."

Grimes understood his own limits. He would go ahead and do as Bimji wanted. He would not test the Asian's intentions nor take any chance with what the police believed. From his pocket he took the crumpled sheet of instructions that the dead man had given him and checked it like a shopping list. Bimji nodded with every detail, a ring of sunlight slipping down his oiled hair with every nod. The Asian pressed his hand to his forehead. "The only thing that will be different now is that I will meet you myself on the beach to wait for my brother's dhow. You will deliver the money directly to me. We will travel there separately. I recommend that you go by road. I will take the overnight train to Mombasa from Nairobi. Do you understand?"

Grimes nodded.

"Do not underestimate me. If you choose to desert me, I will still be able to supply the authorities with the location of Mr. Moguru, even if I am not in Kigeli."

Grimes took the paper with the instructions and was about to toss it into a wastebasket when he thought better of it. He lit the crumpled wad of notepaper and dropped it onto Bimji's polished table. It flared briefly and crumbled to ash. There was a faint, sweet odor of melting wax. Grimes brushed the remnants to the floor.

The Asian kept his eyes fixed out the window, his hands clasped behind his back against the silk of his *kurta*. "There is one more thing, Jonathan. A policeman has been looking for me, a tall man with a suit that does not fit properly. He has been asking questions. I suggest you be careful."

"I'm not going to say anything, Bimji."

"I know."

Grimes gave him the finger as he walked out the door. Behind his back, of course. It was a senile thing to do. He felt he was aging prematurely. I will become a master of hidden gestures, he thought to himself. And I will do what I am told.

BIMJI MADE HIS own preparations to leave. He packed an old leather suitcase that had been left at the hotel during the Mau-Mau emergency by a British correspondent who never called for it. He told his niece, the girl with the gleaming dark eyes who cooked for him, that she would return with him to her parents' house in Mombasa. She took the news with the same equanimity she had shown when she first learned she was to become her uncle's house servant. She busied herself gathering a stack of tiffin cans from the kitchen to carry food for the long car journey to Nairobi and the train ride that would follow.

The Asian went to his store, gathered his employees around him, and told them he was taking a long trip. Snapping the bank's paper band from a teller's stack, he passed out hundred-shilling bonuses. They would take care of the business until he decided what to do with his holdings in Kigeli.

They were good workers. For the most part they did not steal from him. They kept their silence about what they saw inside his house, and in turn he made an effort to exercise some discretion in what he let them see. He did not need to spin around the Kigeli workers the elaborate web of obligation with which it was necessary to keep men like Grimes or Landers next to him. The Kigeli were, after all, in their own land. He knew some of them perhaps did not respect him, but because he was their employer they would not betray his secrets. It was a matter not of respect for him, but of respect for themselves, an inbred rectitude. It would not be a proper way for a Kigeli man to behave.

Bimji knew he himself did not have that sense of duty. He could cheat the Kigeli without guilt. He could beg and swindle and cajole African, European, or Asian. It was the privilege of his foreignness, the anarchy of exile he knew he shared with Grimes and Landers. And with Moguru, who had tried to swindle him, Moguru who was Kigeli but had learned to become a stranger and whom Bimji, in a moment of great fear, had had to kill.

Bimji waved the memory from his mind. He could smell the sweetness of the snacks his niece was preparing for the trip. If they left now, they would be in Nairobi by nightfall. They could stay and see the city the next day before catching the Mombasa train. Bimji had a friend in Nairobi, a man who had known Bimji's father. The man was blind now, his teeth blotched from years of betel. But his memory was clear, and he could tell the girl tales of her grandfather who had worked with a pick on the train line and who had carried homesick memories of India with him into the savannah. He would tell her how Bimji's father, remembering the parading elephants of his childhood that marched at festivals—their heads draped in garlands, wrapped in silver—had tried to tame an elephant near one of the railway work camps. The animal was an orphan, and Bimji's father had set out a bucket of water in the dry land and gathered brush to feed the creature. As the other workers watched, the elephant accepted the food and water. But when, in triumph, Bimji's father stepped up to pat the animal's trunk, the elephant smelled his strangeness. Terrified, he kicked the bucket over. Knocking the man down and breaking the bones of his hand, the beast ran off in fumes of dust to the thorn trees of the open country.

The old man in Nairobi would say that Bimji's father was always expecting too much of Africa, but that he had a good heart. For your grandfather's sake, he would tell the little girl, you should have such a heart, too.

An expectant heart, Bimji thought, was not one of his own difficulties. He looked about the private rooms for things to take with him. There was little. He had made a hotel of his house, reserving the best views and the quietest places for strangers. What he would take was eminently movable. The cash from the last load of Landers's hides and skins he would take himself. The rest would be carried by the American.

Once free on the ocean, Bimji could alight where he chose. There was money to be made in the ports of the Arabian Gulf. Perhaps another hotel or store. He had heard that cinemas were an attraction. The aristocrats of the sheikdoms were willing to pay for private showings of the films that the Islamic censors would not permit at the public theaters. A hotel with a comfortable screening room, refreshments available, discretion assured, in Qatar or Dubai. Bimji knew he would survive. Once free on the ocean.

There were only two obstacles now: the tall policeman who was asking questions and whoever had shot Landers.

Bimji's heart began to quicken, touched by fear. He could do little about an unknown assassin. Without a hint of a reason, a whisper of an identity, there could be only general precautions. He would protect Meera, his niece. He would take care that they not be alone. They would stay in crowds, in public. In Nairobi and on the train ride to Mombasa, they would move about and not stand still. All easy things to do while traveling in cities.

There was really nothing to be afraid of. An old man and a young girl would travel to the coast, gliding down from the highlands on the steel rails his father had laid down in the savannah sun. Times were different now. The wild animals were all kept in the parks.

CHAPTER VIII

ELLEN WAS FOND of Grimes. She even thought she loved him. But there was something exasperating about him. At crucial moments he wasn't there. He evaporated.

She could always sense when the uneasiness came over him. A word she spoke or a look would suffice, anything that might threaten to draw from him an admission. If she said or did something that—even for a moment—assumed too much of an intimacy between them, then Jonathan seemed to feel defenseless and the disappearing act would begin. His eyes would close to her. He would sit at the edge of the bed and answer questions with the noncommittal kindness heads of state use when they are interviewed in their palaces by TV newsmen.

In those little moments of domestic terror even Norwood, Ellen's cat, spooked Jonathan. The huge, marmalade tom would rub his muzzle against Grimes's thigh, and Jonathan's skin would freeze in goosebumps. He became, literally, ticklish all over, and he curled away from loving touches. It took all the gentleness that Ellen had to coax Grimes open again, a nonpossessive gentleness that Grimes found saintly and Ellen found wearying.

But today was different. Grimes was all there, and he was in trouble. He had hitched up the mountain road in the middle of the day when Ellen was still at the blackboard. Through the wire grating of the classroom window she saw him arrive and then could see him pacing on her front porch, his pack on his back, smiling and frowning to himself as if he were rehearsing in his mind the lines to a particularly impassioned play.

When the school clerk's hand bell signaled the end of the day's classes, she rushed over to Grimes. Without speaking he held her to him, full of vulnerability and a hard-on. Inside, on the thin mattress, surplus from the convent nuns, he told her a crazy story about murders and black money. There was nothing protected now in his eyes. It was all true, and he was afraid. He wasn't sure what was going to happen, and he wanted her to know if anything did happen. He wasn't asking for advice, he said, because he didn't think he would be able to take any. He wanted comfort and a kind of witness; he wanted someone who would be able to explain.

They made love in daylight, as they always did. The priests and nuns ran Ellen's school and the clinic and church attached to it. She could go down the road to Grimes's school overnight, but when he came to Kongoru their meetings had to be ambiguous enough so that they could be considered—at least nominally—as long afternoon teas.

Not that they were particularly decorous. The convent bed was not made for this sort of thing. It groaned and heaved. The springs shuddered. Only Norwood's monumental placidity enabled the huge cat to sit through it all at the foot of the cot, licking from his paws the memory of last night's field mice and smiling at the man and woman twining next to him.

As Ellen and Grimes rested, Ellen turned down the Rolling Stones tape spinning on the cassette player—their tea music. The lovemaking had drained some of Grimes's apprehension from him. The touching of their hips, Ellen's closeness, calmed him.

"Does all this surprise you?" Grimes asked her.

For a moment, Ellen studied Grimes's open, irredeemably Midwestern face—the blue eyes, the sandy hair—then kissed him gently on the forehead.

"No. Not really."

It was not the answer he wanted, but it was the true one. Grimes was the sort of man who took chances, but never with ease. Risk was not natural to him. When he gambled too much, or drank too much with the wrong people, it was as if he were daring himself. It was never done without sweating, without a tangle of fear in his intestines. His dreams were of an easy recklessness: a boy's admiration for the friend who can climb a cliff or walk the top of a fence without hesitation, not because he is so confident of his balance that he does not consider falling a possibility, but because falling itself holds no terror for him. But in Grimes's mind, he had always seen the broken leg. He did stupid things, dangerous things, in order to limit the territory of his fear.

68

To be reckless with a mind full of apprehension, Ellen knew, was the most perilous kind of recklessness. No amount of trouble that Grimes might have fallen into would have surprised her.

"I think you should just go ahead and do what Bimji says. Try to do it quickly. And safely. Then stay down at the coast. Get someone to teach your classes for a week and soak it off in the ocean. It will melt away, Jonathan, I know it will."

Ellen softly rubbled the muscles of Grimes's shoulders. Even after the lovemaking they were still tight. Slowly they began to ease.

They dressed in silence. Then, opening the window, they had a cup of tea and looked down at the stream that ran at the bottom of the lush ravine behind Ellen's cinder-block house. Grimes donned his pack again. They kissed, and he was gone. He thought it best to go out the back door, hiding as much from the priests and nuns as from any tracker.

Ellen opened the windows of her small house, the rusty latches creaking. An afternoon breeze blew down from the mountain through the wire gratings. The gratings were there to protect against thieves, though as far as Ellen knew there had never been a thief at Kongoru. Ellen never locked her doors even when Jonathan visited her. She held an informal office hour at home in the late afternoon, after the girls had had their daily sports session. The least shy of the students would come in and ask Ellen questions about their class assignments or about Life in America. It always sounded in capitals. Of what are the beds made in America? Where are the cattle kept? What qualifications are required to teach secondary school? Is it ever this hot in America? Is it ever this cold?

Some of the students refused actually to cross the threshold of Ellen's house. Other, earlier teachers had made that taboo, but Ellen found it hopelessly awkward to stand on the porch for twenty minutes discussing how old people are treated, differentially, in Kigeli and Albuquerque. Her legs grew tired. She had to keep tightening her calf muscles to keep the blood circulating; so eventually she compromised with the accepted decorum and set two chairs and a small table out on the red, waxed cement of the porch.

When Ellen turned around from the window after Grimes had left, Sister Anna was sitting in one of the porch chairs. The sister was a short, extremely dark-skinned woman from the country's Central Province who was in training to be a nurse at the hospital. Anna was not a Kigeli, and Ellen sometimes thought the other nuns had snubbed her into an excessive timorousness. She might have been sitting there for fifteen minutes, afraid to knock, waiting for Ellen to notice her. For an instant, Ellen worried that Anna had been on the porch while Grimes was still there. Then she dismissed it. The sister would surely have left if she had heard voices inside. Anna had the instincts of a hare.

But she had not left. She was sitting there with her hands clasped tightly against the black of her robe.

"I have something to tell you, Ellen." The young nun looked around, scanning the hillside. There was no one else to be seen except the students at the top of the ridge, black silhouettes chasing a soccer ball. "It is a private thing. It is about a man."

Ellen nodded and asked her to come inside. As she showed Sister Anna in, Ellen glided a hand back through her hair and gritted her jaw a moment. After Grimes, she didn't know if she was ready for this. First her lover was telling her that someone was trying to frame him for murder; now a nun wanted to make confession.

It was not at all clear what Sister Anna wanted to confess. Ellen did not ask if she were pregnant. She really didn't know what to ask. Ellen was amused, even somewhat flattered, that she was regarded by the Kongoru nuns and novices—whether because of her status as a sophisticated foreigner or merely her nonreligious-ness—as the local expert on sexuality. But she had no experience in the close interrogation of sisters. She let Anna do the talking and was thus resigned to a certain amount of stammering and silence.

Anna said she had been seeing a man from her home village on the weekends that she paid visits to her family's *shamba*. He had at first said he wanted to ask her questions about the church. He then told her he was in love with her and that she should leave the church for him, to become his wife. His second wife. The man was Protestant, nominally. He was also a polygamist. While all the local Christian groups disapproved of the practice, some were more complaisant than others, assuming that economic realities coupled with moral suasion would make the custom die out. In the next generation. There was no virtue in disrupting the lives of families already in existence.

Anna had told him no. He said he would kill himself. He showed her a knife he had saved for the purpose. Anna did not consider this an idle threat. The man came from a clan known to be crazy.

Ellen asked what Anna had done.

70

Anna was evasive, but she cried a great deal.

"You must see his letters to me. They are not fit letters for a man to send a woman. He does not take them to the convent. He leaves them at my door in the night, or he has his daughter give them to me. She is a student at the primary school. He is an older man, you see."

Ellen took a handkerchief from her dresser and wiped the tears from Anna's eyes.

"You would understand if you saw the letters."

"I am sure I would." Ellen felt a gush of sympathy. It was warmer, less detached than she might have suspected, as if the tension left by the lovemaking with Grimes had dammed up some feeling that Sister Anna's story was releasing. Whatever guilt the girl was feeling, this trouble, unlike Grimes's, was not something she had brought down on herself. And she was just a girl. She could not be more than eighteen.

"I will bring them to you, Ellen. But not here." She gave one of her hare's glances again. "You could take me for a drive, and I would show them to you."

Ellen agreed they would meet at the entrance to the hospital grounds in fifteen minutes.

Ellen spent the necessary ten minutes warming up the engine of her 1959 Morris. She had inherited the car from a Peace Corps agricultural worker who had managed a ranch project near Isiolo and used the Mini in lieu of a trained cattle horse. He could generally lift it out of ditches by himself. It had been through a lot.

She lurched the car into gear, pulled painfully up the hillside in front of her house, and climbed over the shoulder of the long mission drive. Anna was waiting at the gate. Her shoes polished gleaming black, her hands clutching a neat manila folder at her waist, she looked to Ellen as if she were going for an interview at an employment agency.

She hopped quickly into the Morris when Ellen stopped. Anna was familiar with the car. She held both the inside and outside handles tight when she slammed the door and with a movement of her heels made sure the cardboard patches covered the holes in the automobile's floor. Anna then gave Ellen a bewildering series of directions: an uphill left, a downhill right through a series of sharp ravines, an uphill left again where they heard a colobus monkey scream in the treetops, and then another left until they were on a narrow country track carved out of red clay, with, here and there, smooth, even patches of tea plantings allowing squares of sunlight through the trees.

As they drove farther along, Sister Anna nodded in soft agreement with the scenery. "This is a quiet place," she said. She did not open the folder on her lap.

Around a leaf-darkened bend in the track, Ellen suddenly jammed on the brakes. There was a Land Rover with a closed canvas top blocking the center of the steeply banked road. One wheel had spilled off the edge of the graded dirt and was spinning wildly, sending a blinding cloud of red dust into the air. It coated the Mini's windshield and filtered through the rolled-up windows.

"I'll see if I can help," Ellen told Anna. The American woman coughed, then, wrapping a handkerchief over her mouth, she jumped out of the car and ran around behind to the passenger side where the air was clearer.

The late afternoon shadows and the dark of the forest cover obscured the Land Rover's driver as much as the swirling dust. Ellen heard the repeated whine of the accelerator, a buzz that rose in pitch and volume to the sound of a power saw and then died away with each of the driver's attempts to gain traction.

Ellen could barely stand it. The strange day had already given her a headache. The engine's screeching and the whine of the tire against the soft clay scraped against the inside of her skull.

"Don't do that," she yelled into the roar. "You're burning the rubber." Then she stopped, a twinge of embarrassment. She had no right to assume the driver spoke English. She tied the handkerchief around her face. Feeling slightly ridiculous in her bandit's mask, she stepped over to the wobbling vehicle that was spewing dirt like a dredger.

There were four nuns in the car huddled around the driver, two in front, two in back. They must be from Kongoru, Ellen thought, although she didn't recognize the Land Rover. Then, as she walked to the front door, she saw the yellow painted letters and the free-hand cross drawn on the panel.

Poor Sister Anna, she had come all the way up here to get away from them, and now a carload were shipwrecking themselves in the middle of her privacy. The sisters, their backs all turned toward Ellen, still were leaning over the driver's seat. They apparently didn't notice Ellen through the noise and haze. A fat lot, mused Ellen, looking at the short, broad backs of the nuns, what seemed like an acre of black linen under the bobbing white wimples, an occasional glimpse of dark skin at the neck.

72

She knocked on the passenger side window once, then again. Finally the nun nearest her turned around to face Ellen. She had dark, bloodshot eyes, magnified by thick, rimless spectacles. And she had a submachine gun in her hands, pointed at Ellen's heart.

The nun told Ellen to clasp her hands behind her neck. Another of the sisters came around the car holding an automatic pistol and tied a rope quickly about Ellen's hands and neck. Any strong movement of her arms would pull the cord tightly around her throat.

Ellen called out Sister Anna's name, but the young nurse remained mute and still by the side of the Morris. By now the Land Rover had completely emptied, and the four women stood in a semicircle around Ellen, her back forced against the side of the vehicle. One of the nuns stepped forward and frisked her. The hands she felt were male, the roughness was a man's, and Ellen was aware of the brief but lingering delight they took in the contour of her body. As the four spoke to each other in an African language that Ellen did not understand, she realized that at least two of the other nuns were also men.

"Who are you?" Ellen asked in Kigeli with a voice harsh from fear and dust and the scratch of the rope at her larynx. The nuns made no reply. She tried again in English. No answer. Then in Kiswahili. The tallest of the male sisters waved his pistol at her.

"Funga mdomo, mama." Shut your mouth, woman. Ellen smiled. For what it was worth, she had established a medium of communication. They were not local people, and they did not understand, or choose to understand, English. She opened her mouth to ask a further question, but before she had begun the tallest sister slapped her in the face, the long nails of his hand raking Ellen's cheek. With the best aim she could muster under the circumstances—given her tied hands and the ambiguity of the nun's robe—Ellen kneed the man in the testicles.

The blow was accurate. The nun stumbled, clutched himself, and bent over the ground in a moan, the folds of his wimple dragging in the red roadbed.

The short nun with the eyeglasses grabbed Ellen and pulled her toward him by the rope. As the sisal burned into the skin of her neck she started to choke, as if she were caught in the middle of a cough she could not complete. The nun twisted the rope tighter in his hand, and Ellen's head sank toward the ground. The last thing she remembered before losing consciousness was the red-soiled hem of the nun's robe and the glimpse of a pair of sneakers.

73

Then the light in Ellen's vision shrank to a circle and went out.

The small nun told the others to throw the American into the back of the Land Rover. Then he knelt over the man still holding his groin in pain. The other nuns picked Ellen up and dumped her over the vehicle's tailgate, wrapping her loosely in a tarpaulin that stank of mildew.

"Wait!" There was a quick, worried scream from Sister Anna, still standing alongside Ellen's car. She ran over to the Land Rover, drew back the tarp, and extracted an elephant hair key ring from the American woman's pockets.

As Anna stepped back from the Land Rover, she turned to the short nun who had twisted the rope around Ellen's neck. The man had thrown back the top of his robe to reveal the broad lapel of a blue suit.

"Where is my money?" Anna asked in Kiswahili.

The short man laughed, then took three bills from the large pouch that hung in the folds of his habit.

"You won't harm her any more, will you?" Anna clutched the bills, afraid.

The small man dismissed the nurse with a brief wave of his hand, as if he were swatting a fly. "We will follow instructions."

Anna lowered her eyes, then walked back to the car. The Morris gave its usual wretched coughs and whines, then caught. Anna turned the car carefully in the narrow roadbed and disappeared down the hill. She had left the empty manila folder fallen on the shoulder, half-buried in the soft, crimson clay.

The tall man who had slapped Ellen had recovered from her kick. He stood up and slammed the Land Rover's tailgate shut so violently that he cut the flesh of his hand. The sight of his own blood froze him for a moment. Then he wiped his hand on the darkness of his robe and called to one of the others. They propped the vehicle up against their backs and lifted the rear wheels onto the roadbed. Glancing at the gas gauge, he sighed, then emptied a jerry can of fuel into the tank of the Land Rover. The jostle and the fumes started to revive Ellen. She coughed and spat and seemed about to scream until one of her abductors jammed the handkerchief that still dangled around her neck into her mouth.

"You will only grow tired, mama," the man said, "and that would be uncomfortable for you. I am afraid you have a long safari. I would recommend you sleep." And then he began a sweet, cooing song, his voice low and smooth and rhythmical. The rest of the men knew

74

the lullaby, too, and after a wave of small laughter they joined in, their voices rising in the sudden nightfall like the warmth of a campfire as they drove down the mountain road, across the savannah to the distant sea.

CHAPTER IX

THE MORGUE AT the district hospital was inadequate. The refrigeration equipment by itself was sufficient, but it had to accommodate the irregularities of the generator. As a result, the smell was unfortunate and intense. Okiri knew that as a policeman he was supposed to be accustomed to this, but he was not, and he could feel his stomach lifting slightly with each inhalation. The doctor pointed over to a low cot, of the type the Indians call a *charpoy,* on which Landers lay, stiff and pale.

The doctor had given Inspector Okiri a pair of latex gloves to wear. They were still warm from the sterilizer. Okiri did not want actually to touch the corpse if he could avoid it. Thankfully the doctor, an officious Luo who had just come from medical school, was more than happy to take charge.

"The bullet wounds are two in number. One here, adjacent to the sternum, directly through the heart. The second in the cranium." The doctor pulled back the sheet with each exposition. "I removed both bullets. Mr. Landers was shot from the front at point-blank range." The Luo rubbed his latexed hands together and somewhat vaguely cracked his knuckles. "I am, of course, willing to testify whenever necessary. Provided of course there is sufficient notice. My responsibilities here are quite pressing. I . . ."

"That may not be necessary, Doctor."

The physician betrayed a touch of disappointment. "Really? I would think scientific evidence would be of paramount importance in a trial."

"There isn't anyone to try yet."

Okiri didn't know what to do with his hands. He started to gesture, then stopped. The gloves intimidated him. He kept holding

77

his hands up limply, as if they were two fish he was thinking of buying.

"But of course there will be? I have great confidence in the abilities of our police."

"That's wonderful," Okiri said. "I don't."

"But you are a policeman?"

"Exactly. That's why I am not so confident."

"Ah, I see, a joke. Very good. Very fine." The physician had not encountered professional self-doubt before. He also did not want to contemplate losing his chance at the witness stand. Okiri thought him an idiot but then pulled himself back. He was thinking everyone an idiot lately, and it worried him. Perhaps, as the German road engineer had suggested, he should take up boxing. He needed a disciplined way of slugging people.

"You will wish to see the bullets?" The doctor was as obsequious as the Arab storekeepers in Nairobi. He had lowered his voice and was leaning over toward Okiri, which—since Okiri was nearly a foot taller than the doctor—not only was unnecessary, but made the smaller man hard to hear.

"Please."

They returned to the doctor's office, and the Luo happily presented Okiri with the two bullets bobbing in a specimen jar full—for some reason—of alcohol, as if they were someone's particularly interesting kidney stones. "The priests brought me some cartridges as well, from the path. But they are not . . . medical evidence."

"Actually, they'll be more useful to me."

"Really? As you wish."

For the doctor's sake, Okiri held the jar up to the light above the table, then, somewhat guiltily, examined the spent casings. He recognized the bullets immediately. They were .300 caliber, of the kind used by the Schmeisser machine pistols that the government issued police inspectors with the appropriate clearance, the kind of gun he himself might have gotten in Nairobi if he had been willing to do the paperwork.

"Are they all right?" Okiri's pause disturbed the doctor. "I hope I have not done anything inappropriate, Inspector. I have not done this sort of thing before. I am only a recent graduate. I—"

"They are fine, Doctor, wonderful specimens."

The doctor regained his smile.

"In fact, they are the best bullets I have seen removed from a corpse in all my years on the police force."

The man's stethoscope wagged with pride. "I presume you are an experienced man?"

"Three years in my present position, Doctor. May I keep these?"

Somewhat disappointed in Okiri's seniority, the Luo lowered his eyes and nodded.

The inspector moved to put the bottle in the pocket of his jacket, but thought better of it. He unscrewed the cap, emptied the alcohol into the doctor's sink, then put the bullets and the cartridges in an envelope, returning the empty jar to the physician.

"You may keep the bottle, Doctor. Please give us a full report of your autopsy. And Doctor"—Okiri gave his best impression of the authority of the state—"let nothing escape your eye."

Okiri walked out the door. The doctor, sighing, grabbed a boxful of empty bottles from the shelf and returned down the hall to Landers's gray corpse.

OKIRI REBUKED HIMSELF as he drove back to town. It wasn't the doctor's fault he was irritated; he had been annoyed ever since Nairobi had called the local police and told them that he should handle the hunter's murder. He felt it was neither his case nor, more important, his type of case. And it left him in some confusion as to what his priorities were: to continue his pursuit of Bimji's misdealings—the stolen gasoline, the hints of poaching and bootlegging—or to find Landers's murderer. Kariuki, the chief inspector, was completely unpredictable. There was no way to tell which case he would consider more important until he berated Okiri for picking the wrong one.

Okiri mistrusted his intuition that the peculiar hitchhiker of the night before was connected to both Bimji and Landers, since it so neatly solved his dilemma of what to do next. The evidence, such as it was, might be nothing more than a geographic accident. The hunter had been killed on the mountain. Okiri had picked up the hitchhiker near where the summit path joined the mountain road. That placed the little man with basketball shoes near the right area of the mountainside a few hours after the crime must have taken place. Unfortunately, there were at least five thousand other people who lived and farmed just as close to the mountain path. But they had not been spying on Bimji.

Okiri had no idea why the man who murdered Landers should want to spy on Bimji. The only direct connection between Bimji and Landers was that the hunter got drunk a lot at the Indian's hotel bar, the same bar the hitchhiker had been observing the night before.

Okiri had lost the man somewhere in the forest. It was dark and muddy, and dense brush is not the best terrain for a tall man to run in without getting his eye poked out. Besides, the inspector was not a tracker, at least not that kind. Tracking was a skill the police training institutes restricted to park rangers and antipoaching squads.

However, Okiri had other methods at his disposal. A cousin of Ron Richards had seen the enigmatic hitchhiker the afternoon the inspector arrived in Kigeli. He'd said he had seen him in town at least twice before. The little man had come into the Coffee Hotel (not Bimji's—it seemed only Europeans, Asians, and provincial government officials went to Bimji's) with Isaac Moguru, a schoolteacher. The hitchhiker, who was more elegantly dressed at these times, always paid for Moguru's meals and beer.

Okiri decided to pay the schoolteacher a visit.

HE DROVE THE few miles out to the secondary school along the road that wound past the prison. The car tracks ended by a wooden gate. On the top of a low ridge behind a soccer field he could see the teachers' houses. The school clerk, a gnomish man who, by the way he squinted at Okiri, seemed to be wearing spectacles ground to somebody else's prescription, pointed out Moguru's house as well as the fact that Moguru was out of town.

The schoolteacher's wife was there, though, hidden behind a stack of brown exercise books and absorbed in a copy of *The Prisoner of Zenda*. Okiri knew the book but was embarrassed to mention how. He had read it in the library at his own secondary school—in Longman's Simplified English. He had had unpleasant experiences in the past discovering which scenes were left out of such abridgments.

Moguru's wife was extremely tired. She seemed relieved to have a caller.

"He left me the term examinations," she said and then excused herself to fix the inspector a cup of tea.

Okiri settled himself in as best he could in a short, straight-backed chair that clearly had been taken from one of the school classrooms. The house was a drab cinder-block cottage constructed according to the standard official plans for government-supported schools. Okiri's brother, who was a history teacher near their home, lived in one identical to this. The Mogurus' individualization of their home was restricted to one wall—painted a bright green—from which a single shelf protruded. The inspector noted four objects on the shelf, neatly and evenly spaced: a green plastic bowl filled with bananas; a portrait photograph of Moguru and his wife, taken against one of the painted backdrops of potted palms that local photographers always had available; a small carved stool; and a Coca-Cola bottle plugged with straw.

A clear liquid filled the Coke bottle, with a thin, long-undisturbed layer of sediment at the bottom. Okiri could not resist. While Mrs. Moguru clattered in the kitchen, the inspector walked to the shelf and picked up the bottle. He shook it slightly. The sediment rose an inch or two, like the peculiar snowfalls Okiri had seen in souvenir paperweights from temperate zones. Okiri sniffed at the top. Nothing. He pulled the straw loose and took a deeper breath.

"The ocean, Inspector. A gift from my husband." Mrs. Moguru set down her teapot. "From one of his journeys. See?" She took the bottle from Okiri and poured out a tiny bit of the fluid into one of the painted teacups, as if it were an ancient cordial. Okiri brought it to his lips.

"Salt water," he said and grinned, tasting the stale tang of the sea.

"I have never been there myself. Just the pictures in the books. So Moguru brought me this as a surprise, a souvenir." She smiled and glanced at the pile of exercise books she had cleared from the table. "He is a man who likes to give gifts."

"Where is your husband now?"

"At his *shamba,* I think."

"Where is that?"

"In the Nyarene Hills. It is land left him by a clansman who had no children."

"Does he go there often?"

"Maybe once, twice a month. Usually on the weekends so he can attend to his classes, but sometimes like this, in the week. He has many obligations, you know. Because he has education and this job, the rest of his family depends upon him. If there is a problem at the farm, they send a boy down on the bus to town and call for Moguru. He is a judge for the family."

Okiri sipped the rich tea, the milk frosting his dark lips.

"Do you expect him back soon?"

There was a moment of silence while the woman brought her

cup to her face. She was holding it in both hands, as if she wanted its warmth.

"I don't know when he will come. When he goes like this—when they call for him—he does not tell me. A few days, a week."

Country time. Okiri was irritated. He would not be able to wait a week to ask Moguru about his friends.

"Perhaps you can help me," he said. Okiri described the small man he had seen the day before to the teacher's wife. Had she ever seen her husband with such a man?

For an instant she stared out the window, her gaze caught by something Okiri could not see. The inspector repeated his question.

"He has a cousin," she said finally. "One of those who comes to Moguru with quarrels to settle. A short man. But very strong. His hands are too big. They are as big as . . ." She searched for a moment. Then her eyes settled on Okiri. "They are as big as yours."

She refilled the teacups then reached to the shelf on the green wall. "He is also a man with presents. He gave us this stool. He said he carved it, but I think he is too rich a man to make things himself."

Okiri ran his fingers over the thin, curved legs of the stool. *Samba* wood, the hitchhiker had called it. Perhaps he really was a carver.

The woman smiled. "You have such wood in your part of the country?"

"No. We have fewer trees than you Kigeli have. But I have heard of it. Your husband's cousin mentioned it to me."

"No trees? Where do you hide?"

"We don't. We learn to run quickly."

She laughed, a quick, charitable laugh, and ran a forefinger along her lips. "So you have met Isaac's cousin?"

"Yesterday. He was . . . visiting the town. You said he was a rich man. Does he have business here?"

"Probably. He works for the government, but he owns land here. He is one of those people who attract land. He says he knows Mathenge, the Home Minister. When there is a new settlement scheme, he always seems to get a few plots for his own. He opens the minister's car door for him, and he gets a new *shamba* for his troubles.

"With his position, he could help Moguru. But he doesn't. He brings my husband a bottle of whisky, makes talk about Nairobi—this minister and that permanent secretary—and expects devotion in return." Again she touched her lips, and paused. "Moguru is the elder, you know. I think the others should show more respect. No matter who their friends are."

"You say he works at the Home Ministry?"

"Yes."

"Do you know what he does?"

"No. Moguru doesn't tell me these things. I don't even know all the man's names. He comes to the door. Moguru greets him, and they go out."

Okiri still held the *samba*-wood stool in his hands. It really was an elegant piece of work, silk-smooth, dancing curves.

Mrs. Moguru stood up. She placed her own hand on the stool's burnished seat. "I will give it to you, Inspector, if you like."

"I couldn't do that."

"Of course you could. It will be something to remember the Kigeli by."

A policeman refusing a gift was practically unheard of. Okiri felt he could not violate tradition, but he had no place to put it. It was too large for his briefcase or a pocket.

"You could tie it to your spear if you had one. But perhaps your belt." The schoolteacher's wife was grinning like a cat. She appeared inordinately eager to give away the hitchhiker's stool. Okiri made a shy half-turn. He unbuckled his belt and slipped it through the fretwork in the legs of the stool. He turned back to the woman, the stool dangling from his waist, underneath the fold of his suit jacket.

"There. Now you are a proper Kigeli warrior."

"You husband won't mind your giving this to me?"

"It is a gift from us both."

Okiri felt sheepish. His awkwardness drove the questions from his mind. Except one. About Moguru himself, not the hitchhiker. He looked back to the cola bottle on the green shelf.

"Why did your husband go to the coast?"

"Business. Buying land again. He said he had to see someone in Malindi who wanted to buy a *shamba* here from him."

"The farmland was here?"

"I think so."

"So why didn't the buyer come here, instead of your husband going there?"

"I don't know, Inspector." Her face was shy and serious again. "Perhaps you should ask my husband these things when he gets back. He does not tell me about his business affairs. All I know about is the work he leaves me when he goes to do these things, not the work he goes to do."

"I will not be here."

"Then I cannot help you any more."

Okiri finished his tea, the stool on his belt rubbing the table as he crossed and uncrossed his long legs. He rose carefully, thanked the woman for the tea, and returned down the hill to the Capri.

The car had attracted a gaggle of second formers in green shorts who were circling it curiously and carefully as if it were a large, unfamiliar dog whose good intentions they suspected but were not willing to try. When a six-and-a-half-foot-tall policeman with a stool tacked onto his belt came up to drive it, they were paralyzed between terror and laughter.

Laughter won. The children shrieked and giggled: gay, intrusive screams. The sound cut through Okiri. It disturbed him somehow, more than criminals' threats. He pushed a boy aside, too roughly, and sat in the driver's seat. As he began to rev the engine, he felt an edge of panic, wildly inappropriate, and then a wave of shame ran through his body. He swung the car onto the dirt road and, as if chased by demons, floored the pedal and sped toward Kigeli town.

CHAPTER X

IN THE NIGHTTIME, Grimes walked the Nairobi streets. A chilly wind blew down from the hills. Watchmen in front of the hardware stores and new car showrooms huddled around small pots of fire, the flames glinting on long rings of earflesh, yellow teeth, faint cheek scars from old ceremonies.

"*Hujambo, rafiki.*"

"*Sijambo. Habari gani?*"

"*Nzuri. Nzuri.*"

Hands rubbed together. Under ancient, baggy raincoats, the old men rocked on their heels like old dinghies creaking at sea. Grimes aroused no notice. He was a white man, well dressed, unexceptional. At a smoking *jiko* he bought an ear of corn with sprinkled kernels, dull yellow and white. The corn had a faint mealy taste under the thin edge of margarine. It sat like paste in his mouth. Grimes swallowed, chewed again, and walked down the darker streets, gnawing on the cob.

At a corner a blaze of flashlights swarmed like gnats beside two tall streetlamps. There were ten Peugeot station wagons—country taxis lined up by their hawkers—about to sail away from the city. All the cars were a French cream, the roofs sparkling in the flickerings of lamplight. But the bottoms of the fenders were smudged, mud-splattered, the tires wet, black and bald, the bumpers missing or rotted.

The drivers offered Grimes their distances and destinations: to the lake, to the sea, back up to Kigeli. Grimes waved them away. Even in the cool night he felt hot. He couldn't stand still. His foot tapped the pavement; his fingers rubbed his temple, his upper lip, the day's stubble on his cheeks. With a soft motion he wiped at his stomach and Bimji's money belt around his waist, testing its presence again and again as if it were a soreness in his intestines.

After five minutes of waiting, a tiny man riding a decayed bicycle appeared near the end of the taxi stand. He blossomed whole, without entrance, like a headlight on a country road. Jockey-sized and gaunt in flapping gray trousers, the cyclist scanned the sidewalks, then pedaled to Grimes. He circled once before jumping off to brake the bike, one tiny hand on the handlebars, one tapping at the American's back.

"It's been a long time, Jonathan. Follow me."

Smiling like a salesman, Mfupi led Grimes down the somber streets, pedaling a lazy zigzag around the American's uncertain walk.

They were back into wooden alleys now: long, propped shacks of boards pressed against each other. They had come one layer farther out and poorer, behind the streets of stone and masonry. Yet these streets were still something above the low, desolate ravines of shantytown beaten tin: the cardboard hovels in black landscapes of soot and garbage that burned down with every cold night, houses that consumed themselves in cooking fires and that washed away and melted like old newsprint in the months of rain. Mfupi's street was an intermediate country, a frontier town of dust and board. They stepped up into a small doorway, the thin dealer lifting the bicycle around his shoulder to stand clear.

Grimes passed an empty room, windowless beside the street entrance. The walls were coated with oil paper and newsprint. A grotesque advertisement for a skin lightener—a pointillist face with tight straight hair, and a thick, armless hand smoothing the newly bleached cheeks—flared in a candleflame's gusts.

Directly above the flame were the portraits of two dead men: John and Robert Kennedy shaking hands in heaven.

"Your friends," Mfupi said, "went to the moon again."

"Is that too often?" Grimes asked.

"Not at all. Myself, I would like to go. But we are a poor country. You will go?"

"I don't think they want me." Grimes fidgeted in the half-light. He thought of snow. There had been a mountain cabin with wooden walls like this and the glow of kerosene. His father had taken him up the mountain, but neither the man nor the boy had been in shape for a climb. Their boots were wet and cold, and the water seeped in through the laces. Both he and his father were tired. But they had each pressed on to please the other, sharing a lukewarm dinner of hash and beans, then falling asleep almost where they sat, folded over the cabin's pine table. Grimes had turned down the lantern and folded a blanket around his father's shoulders. The next morning they didn't try the summit but went down the hillside together, holding hands when the trail was level. For a moment, Grimes saw Landers again, as, leaving that other cabin, he had seen him last: the older man's face hidden, nodding by the fire.

"Do you want a pound, or only some cigarettes?" Mfupi was up a stepladder now, his hand through the ceiling boards.

"Just something for tonight."

"Cigarettes then, a shilling apiece." Mfupi hopped down with his fist clutched around thick, loose reefers. The odor of the marijuana was oily, intense. Grimes felt as if the herb brought its own heat into the small room like a handful of coals. Mfupi handed him two of the reefers. The small man pulled absentmindedly at his earlobe, which bore a faint, raised scar. "You are alone, then, tonight?"

"Yes."

"Your woman is not here?"

Grimes shook his head. "She's back upcountry."

"A pity." A teakettle whistle of wind blew through a chink beside the picture of the Kennedys. Mfupi tracked it down and nailed a torn flap of cardboard over the hole. Satisfied, he took a Bic lighter from his pocket and lit one of the fat cigarettes he had earlier placed on the table. He took a deep breath and steamed the smoke out his nostrils, then passed the flaring herb to Grimes. "You will stay here then. I have friends at mine tonight, and you are a long-term customer."

Grimes held his breath a few seconds. He couldn't leave the city until the morning anyway. It would be better than trying to sleep off his anxiety in some hotel room. He exhaled, leaned back in a plain wood chair, and smiled.

"What do you have to eat?" he asked.

Mfupi laughed, then stood and beckoned the American one room farther into the shanty. As the smoke warmed his brain, an image from the cover of his students' exercise books smiled at Grimes: "ADVENTURE!" it said in poster letters, and from the letters rose the rays of a rising sun.

TWO HOURS LATER, his belly full of beefsteak and *irio,* Grimes felt positively Elizabethan. Mfupi's room was filled with thieves and whores, pickpockets and cutpurses, light-fingered adolescents and red-dressed harlots. Strumpets, Grimes mumbled to himself, rolling the word in his mouth. If he told himself the truth, the strumpets mainly looked tired, sweat stains under their arms. The ragged shirts of the thieves were coated with sweat as well. Grimes suddenly lost his elation. Only he and Mfupi were without the tinge of sweat. The others had to work for a living. He knew the workers-for-a-living were suspicious of him, of his leisure and the color of his skin. Mfupi had to keep vouching for him with every new arrival, depleting his reserve of good will.

"Government work again tonight," said one of the red dresses. "The ivory hunter."

"Mama," said an old lady with worn skin and bloodshot eyes, dipping a ladle into a sawed-off jerry can, "you need a drink."

"Two," Mfupi said, and spilled out a second glass of the bathtub-made banana gin. He had a newly opened cardboard case full of small tumblers, red and blue flowers etched around their rims. He refilled Grimes's glass as well. "Layla is a special friend of our Home Minister, the Honorable Mr. Mathenge. The work is steady but dull."

The old lady with the ladle scratched a twig among her remaining teeth. "I hear it is heavy work."

Layla did not appreciate the comments. "It is better than dragging water from the river three miles every day to a bad man's *shamba*."

The old woman considered. "But two miles? Better than that?"

Layla finally permitted herself a faint grin. "For two miles I would think again."

Grimes listened to the mild argument on the relative merits of hauling water and hauling Mr. Mathenge's ashes. Other alternatives arose from the group: the tight-lipped, tall, blond men from the UN offices; nervous travelers prowling the entrance of the Starshine Club, eyes in the back of their heads for wives or tour guides; Germans who slept too long afterward, taking time; Japanese, the most peculiar of all, grinning, grunting, soft men who tipped too well and whose pale smooth skin was something almost fearful, as if the women were afraid it was too thin, that it would break at a touch like the skin of someone diseased.

The prostitutes' talk was full of lazy speculation, generalizations set upon correspondences. Two women related the buildings in which their clients worked to the shapes and gestures of the men themselves, the eccentricities of tropical office buildings producing adrenaline-soaked white men far from home, and new, villageless, black men—their pockets full of doubtful money so new and so uncertain that they spent it quickly, as if afraid their prosperity would age prematurely and disappear.

Grimes was drunk now. Huckleberry Finn kept fishing in his mind. He was stoned on Mfupi's grass as well, the two intoxications vibrating in his brain like two organ pipes, octaves apart, distinct and inseparable. Huck and Tom were sitting lazy with their poles, talking in the sunlight by the river, the same roving talk as in Mfupi's shanty room, the straw-hatted boys and the thieves and whores roaming everywhere in their speech, loose tongues, talking free.

"Don't cross Mathenge now, Layla." The old woman dipped her ladle once again, and her eyes gleamed. Mfupi seemed to run with the silver liquor to Grimes's empty glass. "He will kill you easy."

"I'm no politician for him to care about."

"But he can hire boys to scare you. You go easy, or you go away."

"Kirera went away." The voice came from the corner, an older man with a faint, curly beard outlining his chin, who had said little before. There were smudges of oil on the lighter skin of his palms held around the flowered glass. "And others, too."

Mfupi hopped over to the man in the corner and nudged him in the arm. "What others? You know something special?"

"I know what I know." He closed his eyes.

"He's always like that," Mfupi told Grimes, "sad about the state of the nation, killers running loose. But he gets by himself. No need to worry for him." Mfupi leaned down to Grimes's ear. "And he don't know much. He says he knows a lot. But he don't know what's not in the newspaper."

"I know the big men in the government steal your land. I know they hunt the poachers and keep the tusks. I know they buy and sell us like bags of maize. I know"—he waved a hand at Grimes— "they pay people like him plenty, and nothing for us."

The old woman chuckled and began to ululate: sending out the long, pulsing keen that was somehow appropriate to both funerals and political rallies. Layla and the other women joined her. The two teenage boys who had been sipping their liquor as if it were sweetened tea started to sing *"Harambee, Harambee,"* the KANU party song, and then the whole, dark room dissolved into laughter. Mfupi sat on the table, his small legs kicking the air in drunken exuberance.

"This old one was a Mau-Mau, Jonathan. You must excuse him. He fought in the Land Freedom Army. But now he doesn't have any land, and he doesn't have any freedom."

The man in the corner put his palms squarely down on his knees. "I've still got a gun, though."

"But it doesn't work, Jonathan. No bullets." Mfupi stared the bearded man down. "Too old and too rusty."

The room laughed again. Grimes turned his face; the talk made him uneasy. He had never before heard an African criticized for his age to his face. But Grimes began, unwillingly, to laugh. The old Mau-Mau with the chiseled beard sat somber, wounded, drunk, the long arms and big hands resting on the chair.

"He looks just like Abraham Lincoln."

There was puzzlement from the room. Only Mfupi showed a sign of recognition. The hustler studied the face of the older man. "Maybe," he said. He did not seem pleased. Grimes did not know whether Mfupi was upset for the old man or for Lincoln. "They both fought for freedom, Jonathan."

"Ah, but Lincoln won."

"Whose fault is that?"

Obviously they could criticize the old man, but he could not, even obliquely. Mfupi, Grimes thought, was now getting pious on him. Africans could be good at that. Piety.

"Fault? Whose fault is it that Lincoln won?" Grimes felt like having an argument. "What's wrong with his winning?"

"Nothing. But what's wrong with this old man's losing? It's not his fault that he lost so the British could keep the price of their farms up. That's not his fault." Mfupi glared at the white man. "Whose side are you on anyway?" he said, but then burst into laughter again and plopped down into a half-broken chair.

"I'm not on anyone's side," Grimes mumbled, suddenly, against his will, taking the whole thing seriously. He resented Mfupi thinking the question was a rhetorical joke.

Mfupi patted Grimes's hand. "Don't worry, friend. It's not important"—he switched to English for an instant—"You are irrelevant to our problems. And I think we here"—he swung his hand to include the curious thieves and whores—"are irrelevant to yours. You are satisfied?"

90

Grimes didn't know whether he was talking about the pronouncement or his half-filled glass.

"Where did you learn that word?"

Mfupi was pleased. "'Irrelevant'?"

"Yes."

"The newspapers." Mfupi quoted, his hand to his forehead to spur the memory. "Such projects are uneconomic. They are irrelevant to our national needs." He tapped the American's knee with his forefinger. "The opposite of 'irrelevant,' Jonathan"—he stared into the white man's eyes—"is 'appropriate,' no?"

"Yes. You're exactly right. It is the opposite."

"If you are irrelevant to our problems, then you are not appropriate to our problems."

"Right. I am not appropriate."

"Good."

"Good. Very good. Can I have another one of those things to smoke?" As he spoke, Grimes steered Mfupi away from English. Grimes was proud of his Swahili. Using it kept him alert. He felt it protected him—and Bimji's money—from his own drunkenness. It is difficult to make inadvertent confessions in a second language.

Grimes watched the old man in the corner rise from his chair. The movements of his limbs were stiffened, arthritic, and Grimes knew in that moment where the resemblance to Abraham Lincoln came from. It was not merely in the old man's face and limbs but in his carriage as well, his motions. Not that Grimes had ever seen Abraham Lincoln move, except in Anaheim, California, in Disneyland, at the age of twelve. There the amusement park engineers had created a Lincoln mannikin out of the flesh-colored plastic Grimes saw later in the artificial bodies that hung in his university's biology labs. Within Lincoln, however, was no replica of organs and veins, but Disney clockwork that ground out the gestures—the hitch of a shoulder, the tremor of an eyebrow—of the Great Emancipator, in time to a tape recording of the Gettysburg Address.

The old freedom fighter in Mfupi's house had the same soulless motion of that automaton president. Though in the African, Grimes knew, the leadenness of the gestures, the sight of the spirit fleeing the body, must come from the mixture of alcohol and age. It occurred to him, in his own haze, that the old man was dying. And for the second time that evening, Grimes thought of his father, sinking into his own, quiet, whisky death.

In memory he stood outside the den, looking on from the hallway, wrapped in the dark. There was a highball glass just beyond his father's fingertips. His father's face was not old. But it was stricken, marked, as if his wife's death were some uncanny natural tempest that he had given up trying to understand: an electrical storm through which he had passed as a helpless witness, himself unharmed. His father had stared at the work brought home to soothe him in its tedium: applications, forms, requests, memoranda—sifting the papers slowly, repeatedly, gently, as if they were not themselves, but the photographs, invitations, and notes of love that he had not the heart to confront.

Grimes saw him, enveloped in sorrow and fatigue, and in his child's mind he could think of nothing to do to express the love he felt, no gesture or word that would perform what he wanted it to do. Made vulnerable by the sleep tugging at his eyelids, the boy had suffered then a defeat such as he had never felt before or since—not even at the moment of his mother's death itself—and had retreated to his room, swallowing his tears.

As he watched the old man who had fought in the forests struggle to stand, Grimes rose from his own chair, flushed with sympathy. "Can I help you?" he asked.

The old man stared at him as if the question were proof of insanity.

"I am defeated by urine," the man said, and walked slowly, stiffly, out the door to the privy.

GRIMES WOKE ALONE. The whores and thieves were gone. Lincoln was gone. Behind the thin partition he could hear water boiling on a *jiko*. Light poured in soft stripes through the gaps between the planks of the rear wall. Mfupi was singing a KANU party song from somewhere beside the bubbling water. There was a pile of yellow rags in the corner of the room, a glint of oil smearing the cloth. Grimes picked one up, wiped it as dry as he could against the denim of his jeans, and pressed it against the sweat beading on his forehead. Running his tongue along the back of his teeth, he tasted his hangover: an alloy of tin and gall. The thought of a bowl of the local gruel for breakfast did not please him.

As he stood erect, he tested the floorboards briefly with his toes, decided everything was as ready as it was going to be, and stumbled toward the cookroom. Mfupi was smoking his first joint of the morning and flipping pancakes in a cast-iron pan as the American stepped across the threshold.

"You are happy?" he asked Grimes, scraping the batter free of the pan with a wooden spoon.

Grimes nodded. "No *posho*?"

"I wouldn't think of it. We must make allowances for guests. Fresh eggs from next door. Listen." Mfupi kicked the wall violently. On cue a rooster crowed. "The proud father." Mfupi beamed and passed Grimes the first plate of hotcakes.

Grimes bit into the steaming disk, dreamed briefly of maple syrup—a recurrent African dream of his, too often flooded away by Lyle's Golden corn muck, a maize-based leprous parody of sweetness—and waited with satisfaction while the pancakes quieted his dancing stomach.

Mfupi studied his patient while he ate. With his forefinger he tapped Grimes lightly on the forehead. "You were drunk," he said. "Very drunk. Normally this is all right. But in your condition . . ."

"My condition?" Grimes felt as if he were pregnant and followed Mfupi's glance down to his waist.

"They wanted to rob you, but I said no. It's my house, and you are my guest." The African gave a quick, sharp laugh and jogged Grimes in the money belt that sat beneath the dark cotton of his shirt.

Mfupi poured cups of tea from the coal-blackened pot. He ground out the cigarette and cradled his cup with both hands. "Can I ask where you're going with that money?"

Grimes was not offended by the question. He felt relief that the fearful caution he had carried with him the night before—until it was demolished by the battering of the tin-bucket gin—had been at once useless and unnecessary. And he felt Mfupi had established a kind of claim against Bimji's black dollars by not taking the money when he had the chance. But he told Mfupi only that it was someone else's money, not his own. He was doing someone a favor. He made no mention of Bimji, of the bodies of Moguru and Landers.

"I'm not telling you any more for your sake, not for mine. Do you understand that?"

"I understand. Don't worry." Mfupi glanced out the window as the woman from next door passed by and waved a broad greeting. Then he put down his teacup painted with roses and held Grimes's hand in the way African men who were friends did. It was something with which the American had never before felt comfortable. But now, for the first time since he had come to Africa, he did not think it strange.

CHAPTER XI

THE GAZELLE RAN alongside the train but lost the race, fell back and down to the dark plain. The moon was gone. Bimji turned his face from the window. His niece's seat was empty, a vegetable croquette half-eaten on her plate. The other diners had left the car, except for a middle-aged European lady slowly spooning sugar into her tea with the care appropriate to gold dust.

Perhaps Meera had gone back to the compartment. The girl was always so quiet. Bimji tucked a small tip underneath his plate and eased himself, somewhat uncertainly, out of the weighted chair. The movement of the train disturbed him, and as he walked down the narrow alley between the tables, he widened his step to steady himself. At a lurch of the carriage he brushed the table of the Englishwoman with his leg. There was no contact, but the mere thought of a violation brought the lady up in her seat. Her pale blue eyes—the color washed thin by age—fixed Bimji with rebuke. But the Asian refused to respond, cleared his throat, and continued past the closed kitchen, through the heaving doorways, into the darkened corridor of the first sleeping carriage.

The porter had sealed the windows facing out toward the savannah, yet the night wind, leaking through old warped joints, still sent swirls of chill into the hallway. Bimji unrolled the sleeves of his linen *kurta,* trying to stretch a few extra inches of warmth out of the cloth. The cold air raised bumps on the flesh of his forearms. As his fingers slipped over the skin he felt a momentary disgust with himself. He was fat. He could offer no excuses. Bimji had always considered his weight an emblem of healthy prosperity. But with age it was being revealed as a subterfuge, an excuse that hid the muscles and strength that time was shrinking inside his body.

He pressed his hands and arms tightly against his belly. From behind the closed compartment doors there was a splash of voices: fractions of argument, the searching static of a shortwave radio, damp coughs. He felt in his pocket for the key to the small padlock on their compartment door—Bimji's own precaution—and found only a cluster of coins. But of course, Meera must have taken it from him.

In spite of the cold wind, Bimji paused on the tiny platform as he passed between the carriages. The darkness of the night held him, as the deep black of the swift clouds blocked voids in the gleam of the starry sky. The thin atmosphere of the high plain made the immense night crystalline, clear. As Bimji gazed at the stars he could see not only their brightness but their colors as well: some were yellow-white, others blue, or the red of pricks of blood. Some sparkled, flaring faintly as if in breath, while others shone cold, mechanical, smooth. His father had told him once of the ancient Indian names for the stars: twenty-seven houses in which the moon lived in a monthly course through the skies. The old man could not remember more than a handful of the words—Bimji suspected he had never known them—but for a day he could speak of hardly anything else, searching in his mind between customers for the old Sanskrit words and leafing through a worn book of universal knowledge, written in English. But that proved worthless: the system was dry and different, the words meaningless. He knew that there were astrologers in Nairobi who could read the sky, and he wrote to one of them for a chart, but as he made no promise of payment, there never came any answer. Often the other Indians that Bimji dealt with relied on such men to plot the dates of weddings and explain the secrets of births and deaths. But although he had sometimes spoken to Jonathan Grimes and other strangers of sons who were students abroad, they were only wishful fictions. For Bimji there had been no births for the astrologers to decipher.

He had been married once, a woman sent from India by his father's relatives. He had been thinner then, though not ever handsome, and when he went to meet the boat in Mombasa he had a street tailor make him a suit jacket of blue cloth with fine, broad lapels. When the girl landed, they walked along the beach with his brother and his wife. The women took the chappals off their feet and ran through the sand. A Gujerati man sold them sweets from a cart. Everything had pleased Bimji.

That evening they took the train up to Nairobi. In the morning they were in the highlands and the palm trees of the coast were gone. The girl wrapped a shawl over her shoulders. The animals running along the tracks his father had laid frightened her. The sky was like that of her home, open and washed with light, but underneath it the land was empty and untilled and she felt as if she were drowning in the sky.

They were married in the city, and she stayed with him in Kigeli. But she was unable to have children. One July, in the month when there is morning fog and the Kenyan farmers go about in old army trench coats, she had a bad attack of malaria. There were not as many hospitals then as now. He tended her himself with the help of another Gujerati couple who had opened a shop near his father's, but within days she was dead. He had no interest in marrying again. He would let his brother fulfill the obligations of family.

The light of the stars began to chill Bimji as much as the wind and he let himself into the next carriage. Meera was standing in front of their closed compartment, her back against the door.

"It's locked, uncle," she said, and wiped her nose. "I had to go to the toilet and I didn't think. So it's locked."

"Where's the key?" Bimji pried at the lock.

"That's what I mean. It's inside. I left it on the seat. I forgot." She searched his face. "I'm sorry."

"I'll try and find the porter. Maybe he can help." Bimji glanced down the hallway. "You stay here and don't leave. Understand?"

The little girl swung her head in acknowledgment. The kohl lining her eyes was smudged by tears.

Bimji didn't want to be put at the mercy of the porter. He would only have to admit that he rigged up the lock in the first place— something probably not permitted—and he would be calling attention to himself. He had convinced himself that the whole move to the sea was something effortless, a smooth glide from his life in Kigeli to a new chance somewhere else. There were supposed to be no obstacles, no interruptions. Now the girl had made a mistake, and though he told himself it was nothing, it triggered within him a fear of all that might still go wrong before he—and the money he had entrusted to Grimes—were safely at sea.

He went first to the back of the train. The cars were all empty, the leather seats where the porters usually waited were turned up against the wall. One of them had to be somewhere. They couldn't all vanish after dinner. He knocked on an unmarked door next to a toilet compartment, once, then again. There was no answer. Bimji slowly eased the door open. Out of the darkness came only the rancid smell of soiled towels. Swearing under his breath, he shut the door, and returned along the rumbling floor to the wagon where Meera waited.

The girl was crying now, her arms loose at her sides. Her head was bowed to her thin chest and every few seconds small tearful shivers wavered through her shoulders. Although in truth the crying was barely above a whisper, Bimji, to make her stop, told her she would wake the other passengers if she kept it up. He searched in his pockets for a small tin of mints. "Here," he said. "They're imported. You'll like them."

The girl took one, hesitated, then popped it in her mouth. Bimji waited for the pulse of her sobbing to ease. "I'm going to go up to the kitchen now. There should be someone there. You'll be good now?"

Meera sniffed a "yes."

"Do you promise?"

"I promise."

"Good. I'll be right back. We'll be asleep in ten minutes." Bimji turned to go.

"There are noises in there, uncle."

"What do you mean, 'noises?'"

"Noises, like mice."

Bimji put his ear against the door. A thin, unpleasant film touched his skin. The solidity of the wood amplified the sounds of the train: the rumbling of the wheels, the strain of the wood and metal vibrating up the column of the door. But he could hear nothing out of the ordinary. Except perhaps something—a breath, scratches against the leather of the seat, or a shifting of papers, wind—was the window open?—just enough of a sound to defer certainty. Nothing really. Clumsily, Bimji squatted down to the level of his niece, their faces together in the corridor's dim light.

"Are you sure, Meera, you locked the door when you went to the toilet?"

"I'm sorry I did it, uncle."

He held her, his weighted hands resting on the bone of her shoulders. "That's not what I mean. Do you remember doing it yourself, closing the lock yourself?"

"I don't know. I'm sorry. I forgot." She rested her head on Bimji's soft chest, the leftover tears damp on the cloth.

"All right. Just wait here. There's nothing to be afraid of." He

98

left her with another of the mints and retraced his steps to the dining car. But the sleeping cars were quiet now. No light leaked from underneath the closed doors. In the dining wagon, the kitchen was empty, the door locked. And ahead were only more of the shadowed, still, Pullman wagons, the compartment doors lettered and anonymous. Bimji felt a pointless urge to shout for a porter, to force the train employees out of their hiding. But he stifled the impulse. Most likely it would only bring the wrath of the sleeping passengers. They probably had no more idea where the porters slept than did Bimji. He was frightened of appearing as what he was: a rather foolish man who seemed to have gone to elaborate lengths to lock himself out of his own compartment.

Finally, again in the night air, exposed on the last narrow platform, he faced the barred, blank door of a freight wagon that rolled between the locomotive with its inaccessible crew and the rest of the train. Bimji took a deep breath in the darkness. Of course there had been nobody in the compartment. This business was irritating, embarrassing, but it was not a threat. The train was not abandoned. People were only asleep.

But someone might have followed them from Kigeli. He was aware of that: the tall policeman, or whoever had killed Landers. Bimji's hands gripped the railing. He could feel the cold air reaching down to the top of his lungs. He knew he had to focus on his obligations, not his fears. He was obligated to his brother to protect Meera. If he could get the girl safely to Mombasa, then he could take care of himself. But he must protect the girl.

Bimji strained to get control of himself. And then he capitulated, swept in a night wind of panic. He ran back through the empty sleeping cars, seeing only shadows and hiding places, corners and suspicions. He passed through the heavy doors and past the tables of the dining car that lay under cloth, softened to featureless shapes like the covered furniture of an abandoned house. As he ran, the dead men, Moguru and Landers, ran with him, stumbling on the dark, unsteady floor of the moving train until he was back before Meera, and all his actions—the patting of a handkerchief on his suddenly sweating forehead, the stale words of reassurance—were deceptions, everything intended to hide from the girl his bewilderment, to keep from her the full force of the exile he felt: his utter separation from this alien land.

He calmed Meera—though by now the girl had calmed herself with sleepiness—and told her he would open the door himself. He leaned his bulk against the latch and pressed. At first nothing moved, then slowly the metal and wood began to give, the ancient screws popping from the grain under the large man's insistence, and the handle and plate fell loose to the floor. He lunged a padded elbow against what remained and pushed through to the inside of the compartment. The noise, which sounded to Bimji like a shattering of worlds, was nothing more than a muffled snap of wood, the cracking of a bough.

The Asian swung the door clear, and it bounced, wounded, against the steel molding of the compartment wall. He took the little girl's hand and led her across the threshold. "See, there's no one inside. No mice." The window was open to the dark Tsavo night, the louvered shutters rattling in their grooves. A half-opened bedroll lay on the seat, the quilted cloth cold to the touch in the draft from the window. Outside, the savannah was velvet black, dark thorn tree shadows making ragged the faint, gray horizon.

Suddenly Meera started, her hand tight on Bimji's. "Uncle, look!" Like the lighting of twin matches, two headlight beams appeared far off on the plain, the dust and the distance making them flicker dimly red. "What is it?" The girl was frightened by the unknown flare of light. Her fingers grew cold as she looked up at Bimji's hooded eyes.

"A car, a Land Rover. There are game lodges out there, you know. For the tourists. It is nothing." Bimji sat the little girl down, then shuttered and locked the window. He propped a suitcase against the door, sat down, then rose again, adjusting his security until they were fastened inside. Bimji was tired. The wash of fear had drained from him with the snapping of the door, and, as he sank into the green leather seat, he was ashamed of the memory of his panic. He closed his eyes. But in his mind, behind the heavy lids, the headlights from the plain flared again, now bright red: red like the stars he had seen from the platform, red like the fire eyes of Kali, the Goddess, in the images his father had shown him as a boy. "It's nothing," he said again, though by now Meera was asleep, unhearing. Alone, Bimji tried to calm his trembling hands. But the loose door still strained against the leather of the suitcase; the shutter of the window still rattled in its grooves.

CHAPTER XII

THE ASIAN HAD gone to Mombasa by the night train. His name, written in green ink, was on the passenger list that Okiri held in his hands. He had been accompanied by a female child. Their carriage was second-class, car 371.

The inspector rummaged through his desk. After knocking a fly off his notebook, he inserted the passenger list in the growing sheaf of loose papers at the back. Then he flipped it open and pondered briefly: Bimji to Mombasa; a green bottle filled with salt water at the house of the absent schoolteacher; a white hunter, perhaps killed by government bullets. A small man with basketball shoes who works *samba* wood, sometimes appears rich and sometimes hitchhikes in rags. A man who appears to be the cousin of the absent schoolteacher and who spies on Bimji. A small man. To Okiri the category "small" was hazy and overly generous. It included most people he met, and he tended to discount its importance. But this man's size was noticed by everyone: in tandem with his arrogance. A little man full of himself.

The inspector flipped a few pages back into the book. Ron Richards at the Starshine had also seen a small man, full of himself, from the Home Ministry. Okiri called Okello—his friend the clerk-typist.

The conversation was difficult. Both men were speaking from desks in open offices; neither was eager to have his neighbors overhear. Okello, in fact, seemed terrified, and soon switched from English to their tribal language, less fearful of being thought a hopeless provincial by his fellows than of having them know he was discussing Section 21. Okello knew the little man only too well.

"His name is Kimathi, brother. It was he who signed out the car to Kigeli that I told you about. I checked the handwriting against some old requisition forms. There is no question. He writes like a Coca-Cola sign."

"If he had the car, why was he hitchhiking?"

"You have not driven a ministry car, brother. Anyway, how should I know? He fancies himself a secret agent. He works"—the clerk-typist stumbled, searching for appropriate words in their language—"he works under blankets."

Okiri puzzled an instant, then gave a grunt of understanding into the phone.

Okello continued. "But he is not as important as he thinks. Sometimes these special missions for the minister are only things you would send a boy for, fetch and carry, you know. Even with a gun."

"He takes a weapon?"

"Always. He carries a gun, wears tight pants, and walks like a rooster. But why is he following you, brother?"

Okiri was slow to answer. The thought had never occurred to the inspector that the little man was stalking him. But once within his mind, it was not that easy to dislodge. "I didn't say he was following me. I am trying to follow him. He is interested in some things that interest me."

"That's a reason for joining a school club together, not for mucking around someone who works for the minister. If I were you, I'd stay out of his business. Kimathi is not as big a snake as he makes out, but he still has venom."

"Has he come back to the office?" Okiri asked.

"I haven't seen him since you left Nairobi. And the car is still checked out. Please be careful, brother. Half of what Kimathi sings is a boast song. What the Section does is not boast at all."

After Okello hung up, Okiri took a warm bottle of orange soda from the office cabinet. The carbonation had long since left it, but the thin, flat liquid was still sweet and that sweetness was what the detective wanted. If he had been in the country still, he would have gnawed a length of sugar cane, pulling on the fibers until the fresh, complicated juice spilled over his tongue. Failing that, he had to content himself with the Fanta and its bitter undertaste of having been aged in plywood. Okiri sat back down in his swivel chair and squeezed his knees under the desk. Okello's assumption that it was Kimathi who was tailing him still disturbed Okiri. He scanned the bland, bureaucratic faces of his colleagues as, licking their fingers at each turning of a page, they sorted through their papers. He ran his hand along the drawers of his desk and tugged slightly to see if each lock was turned shut. Okiri did not like the feeling of being followed, by Section 21 or anyone else.

IT WAS NOT easy learning about the Section. People were reticent. Phone calls were not returned. Okiri knew enough not to be overtly curious; still every time he even got close to the subject there would be a sudden change of weather, a pause, a new cold wind. His superiors began to inquire about the progress of old cases. They checked their new digital watches more frequently in front of his desk. There were no more easy pleasantries.

The documents, the official registers, were no help to Okiri. In frustration, he then did something that contradicted the dutiful sobriety of his training at the hands of the retired colonial inspectors who had manned the police academy even after Independence. He took a simple step: he accepted as true those things that everybody knew but nobody believed. It was as if he had turned a radio up one notch in volume and the noise he had always supposed was merely static became a series of insistent whispers, distinct and understandable. Okiri began to live completely within a world of rumors, of odd, unsteady noises always at the edge of his hearing: the cynical suspicions of shoeshine boys, the confidences of petty crooks, the boasts of unemployed country boys with sudden blossoms of cash in their hands.

The rumors and whispers all told the same story about Section 21 and about the killing of Ezekiel Kirera. Kirera had been the leader of an opposition rump within the ruling party. His credentials were impeccable—he had spent six years in British detention camps before Independence—and his actions, though irritating, were legal. One rainy October morning while giving a slightly soggy speech donating three thousand square feet of corrugated iron roofing to a Rift Valley elementary school, he was shot through the head. The man who killed him fled into the nearby forest. Within two days, Section 21 operatives brought him out to waiting photographers. In the news pictures—dripping rainwater and covered with leeches—he had the look of wounded surprise appropriate to a parachutist who has pulled all the right cords, yet sees no comforting silk ballooning in the sky.

The man with the leeches was brought to trial and hanged. Although the accusation was denied by the Home Minister and even by Jacob Ngano, Kirera's closest associate, the common folklore

103

assumed that Section 21 had not only captured the assassin, but hired him as well. It was a rumor without proof that offered no threat to the Section, yet managed to enhance its reputation. It had a suitably chilling effect on anyone considering becoming an enemy of the state, or of Minister Mathenge.

Ngano in particular had caught the chill. After his colleague's assassination he remained in Parliament, but where once he had given strong speeches demanding accounting from the government's ministers, he was now silent and withdrawn. When needed, he voted with the government. He seemed to have developed an amateur's interest in snakes and was often seen at the National Museum in small back rooms, sifting through sloughed skins and ancient bones.

Ngano was happy to talk with Okiri—in private, though, and in motion.

"I'll pick you up by Jeevanjee Gardens. You'll recognize the vehicle. I've got a zebra van."

"One of the tourist minibuses?"

"Right, with zebra stripes. It makes for anonymity and they're cheap. They've got to sell them to someone."

Okiri climbed up beside the MP shortly after noon. Unlike most politicians, who seemed to plump with office, Ngano was sharp-featured and gaunt. The years in Parliament had honed him. Swinging the car onto the highway, Ngano drove south out of the city toward the Game Park, the Ngong Hills blue in the distance. Spread out along the road, before and behind them, were other black-and-white striped vans filled with their complements of European and American tourists: children with noses pressed to the glass while their parents sorted lenses and filters and waited nervously for the first cry of gazelle upon the horizon.

"Money in the bank, Mr. Okiri. Every one of these vehicles is money in the bank for someone. Not necessarily our countrymen, all of them, but for someone. They come from all over. Why? They could see such animals in their zoos, most of them, and others beside—tigers, polar bears, reindeer—equally strange and wonderful."

"But the animals here are free and wild. They're not locked in cages."

"Not all so free and wild. Their territory is limited. Surely these are not normal lions. They are perfectly used to being stared at by strangers. Their sleep, their mating, their kills, are all circled by these vans and our own idle curiosity. Whether they wish it or not,

104

their whole life is a performance. At best they are music-hall lions. At worst they are merely pets. No, what attracts these visitors, I am afraid, is the pleasant reversal of responsibility. In a zoo in New York or London, the animals are pampered. They are fed. They are guarded from predators. If necessary, if they are immigrants from Africa or South America—a tropical country—they spend the night in warm houses. In the morning people come to clean away their droppings.

"The people, on the other hand, must fend for themselves. They must gather their own food, wipe their own asses. At five o'clock the zoo closes, the gate is locked. The people are herded away to forage on their own. While inside the gates, the keepers present the animals with their assured portions—whatever they need: turnips or raw meat, white mice or eucalyptus leaves.

"But here, Mr. Okiri, the northern tourist has a chance to come to an underdeveloped country. He plunks down the cash for his package tour, and suddenly it is he who is pampered and cared for. His meals, his transport, even his clothing perhaps—a bush hat and a safari jacket—are provided. And he has nothing to do but drive around our roads—in fact, to be driven around by a black chauffeur—and watch these lions, zebra, and elephants. Here, we are not in a zoo. The animals are no longer the chosen, guarded creatures. They no longer have protection from each other. If a zebra's neck is broken by a lion's jaw here, it is not a tragedy. It is a treat for the lucky watchers. But in London there'd be a scandal—someone would be fired.

"The animals must feed themselves here, predators and grazers alike. They eat and breed and multiply until there is too little grass for the gazelles and too few trees for the elephants and only the predators flourish. But as the gazelles and zebra starve, so will the lions. And all the people have to do here is watch, safe in their cars. For all the death and indignity, they have no responsibility. They have not brought the animals here. They are not obligated to them. They have come just to pass the time of day."

Ngano insisted on paying the entrance fee for both of them at the gate to the park. For a moment they were in a traffic jam. As they paused in the line, the exhaust from the car in front drifting against their windshield, a baboon sprang from the side of the road onto the top of the van, the toes of its right leg trailing against the side window. Soon it was lolling over the top, its upside-down head and arm dangling in Ngano and Okiri's vision. Ngano tried to jar it loose by knocking with his fist on the windshield. The baboon

105

merely smiled, its huge grin spreading down from chin to nose. Only when the van started to move did the creature show them its leather-bottomed behind and leap back off into the grass.

As the line of cars freed up, Ngano turned his van down a side track. "We can try the river bottom first. You can still find rhinoceros there." The car rocked along the dirt path, straddling the faint central mound spotted with tufts of the hardier savannah grasses. The MP nodded toward the back seat. "I've got a pair of binoculars if you'd like."

"I'll do fine without them."

"I'd rather you used them, Mr. Okiri." Ngano groped around the rear seat with his free hand. "We are not uninteresting game ourselves."

He passed the Nikons over to the policeman, who cradled them briefly in his palms and lifted them to his eyes. There was nothing at first but a smeared haze of brown and blue, a thin green line separating them in the middle of his vision. He slid his fingers to the focus wheel. A rainbow blur briefly outlined the edges of reality and the ground-glass image coalesced. Okiri saw a low ridge covered with parched grass, a twisted acacia tree at the top—its roots serving to hold a few more drops of water around it in still green grass—and overhead a vast sky, distilled by the magnification into an intense mineral blue.

Suddenly, at the precise line of contact between the sky and the plain, three faint bubbles formed, then spread to color and shape: thin triangles of a dimly yellowed white that quickly specified into long muzzles, narrow heads with tiny bumps of horn, which bobbed and lengthened, until rising over the ridge were three vibrating, muscular necks, long and spotted, weaving in a steady, impulsive rhythm like three fish in clear water, and finally, beneath them, the powerful bodies and legs of three adult giraffe in invisible yoke across the plain.

The animals were not unattended. At the bottom of the ridge Okiri could see two zebra vans split off from the line rolling in the park gate. They gave chase to the giraffe until, drawing even with the animals and slowing to an even pace, they sailed off the binoculars' edge, leaving parallel wakes of brown dust vibrating in the air.

The scene was still again: ridge, acacia tree, and sky. Okiri let the binoculars fall on their strap. He turned to Ngano. "They're just game watchers. I can't see anyone following us."

106

"Good. Please keep checking. I hope you don't mind. I lead a very circumspect life. I am on a kind of probation." He swerved quickly to avoid a sudden gash in the roadway. "You and everyone else are right, Mr. Okiri. Section 21 did kill Kirera. Not only does everyone else say they did, but they say they did. They were happy to tell me that. If you interest them, they are not at all discreet in their threats. In fact, they're quite cheerful. They don't see what the fuss is about as long as they do their job."

"And what is that job?"

"Just what it says on the books: to protect our young state. I suspect they create a space in which Mr. Mathenge and others like him can make their decisions without worrying about pressures from people like ourselves."

Okiri shied slightly. He was looking through the binoculars again. "I'm just a policeman."

"But I suspect you are becoming more than that. You do not merely follow orders, or you would not be talking with me here. And you have promised to keep my identity as a source of information secret, by which I take it you are willing to assume responsibility for what your superiors should and should not know. That is adventurous, whether you find it so or not. There are those who no doubt find it disturbing that you ask them questions about Section 21."

"There are." Okiri spoke almost absentmindedly. He was watching a cluster of vans and cars that circled a group of lions lazing in the sun: a male with a black-fringed mane sitting calmly beside a mother and cubs that sprawled on their backs, bellies toward the heat of the sky.

"Yet you persist."

"I was investigating a case of my own. Section 21 seems to have something to do with it, so I'm asking questions. I'm not out to get anyone." There were four vans watching the lions. Three were filled with tourists, their heads poking through opened sunroofs.

"What was your case?"

"An Indian trader who may be defrauding the government and who some say is a poacher."

"Ah, poaching. Stealing the king's deer. Did you ever notice how many princes and dukes are involved in the international wildlife funds? I think it upsets their ancestral memories. They want to keep hold of their old parks."

Okiri fiddled with the binocular dials. The fourth van seemed

107

empty except for the driver. The man was faceless at that distance, a featureless circle in the lens.

"Poaching is not unknown to Section 21, Mr. Okiri. Perhaps that is your connection with this trader? Mathenge would like the agency to be self-sufficient. If it provides its own funds, it gains independence. It cannot be threatened by disturbing inquiries. The animal trade takes place in remote areas, away from the curious. If it's conducted with sufficient expertise it doesn't even require much in the way of payoffs—not that that would be a problem for the Section."

"Would they consider"—Okiri hunted for a word—"subcontracting the work?"

"Certainly."

"But to an Asian?"

"Unlikely."

Okiri saw the dead hunter again, calm in the makeshift Kigeli morgue. "What about a European?"

"More likely, if he had a special skill or if they had a special hold on him." The MP saw Okiri's mouth and jaw tense into a frown underneath the binoculars. "Do we have a problem?"

The inspector motioned silently to the lone driver's van, which had left the group around the lions and was rumbling along a ridge parallel to Ngano's vehicle.

"I'm developing an urge to see a hippopotamus," Ngano muttered, and veered the van off the track to a tall thicket of reeds that bordered a shallow ravine. Suspension creaking, the vehicle groaned to a stop under a canopy of green. Ahead of them, at the bottom of the ravine, they could make out the brown, complacent stream of the Athi River. Then, as suddenly as he had turned off, Ngano jumped the van into reverse, spun dirt for an instant, and backed up the path.

"Excuse me, Mr. Okiri, that was a mistake. Suspicious behavior, and a dead end as well. Safety is in numbers, isn't it?" The MP chugged the van back up the path toward the herd of zebra vans that surrounded the family of lions. "You see, I panic sometimes. I forget to think things out." For a moment he dropped his gaze. "It was not a way of thinking to which I was accustomed before I met Mr. Mathenge and his friends."

Okiri set down the binoculars as they joined the circle of tourist cars. There were now nearly ten vehicles grouped around the large

108

cats; the closest animal was no more than twelve feet from the tourists. The cubs seemed to pay no mind. They rolled and stumbled across the brown grass. Only the old male, still unmoving, seemed to Okiri to show any apprehension at the encircling humans. Although the slight movement of the animal's eyes was outwardly so calm, so drenched in sun and sleep, that Okiri could not tell if it was the beginning of real anger or merely something external, a play of light.

"You asked me about the coast when you phoned . . ." Ngano turned off the ignition and leaned forward on the dashboard of the van to watch the lions.

"I was wondering if someone working for the Section would have any business there, a reason to make trips."

Ngano rested his head gently on one palm and stared at the black-maned lion. "There is a house there, Inspector, where they have business." His voice flattened with the words, lost the assertiveness that Okiri had heard before. "It is his house, Mathenge's."

"Where is it?"

"A quiet place, north of Malindi a few miles, on a beach. There are no villages nearby and no hotels. They go there for privacy, I assume. They bring people there sometimes." His words slowed again. Ngano had once been a famous orator, and even against the noise of the tourists' snapping shutters, the memory of his voice's resonance drew Okiri into intimacy.

"They brought me there. It was after they shot him, after they shot my friend. Mathenge asked me to come. He said he had information about the killing and that it would be best to discuss it there. In privacy. It is a lovely house, all white like the Arab houses, but made larger, expanded to a European's taste. I'm sure he had some Englishman design it for him. It can be really seen only from the sea. From the road—even at a close distance—it seems to be merely a grove of palm trees.

"In the middle there is a courtyard with a well of white stone in the center. The well is dry. Mathenge sits on the edge of it when he speaks to you. I am sure it is not comfortable, Inspector, but it raises him up above those he speaks to, like a throne.

"They told me they would kill me. There was no subtlety or indirection, just a threat I knew they were completely capable of carrying out. You see, my friend Kirera played games. He was a serious statesman and committed to the people of this country, but he played the games he had learned at our nice colonial school, of politeness, and deceit, and persuasion. He assumed that even men who were evil played games that same way. But they didn't. They just hired someone to shoot him through the head.

"You must understand that without Kirera I had no future. I had his convictions, but I lacked his personal following, and I lacked his courage. So when Mathenge told me to shut up or be killed, I shut up. He leaned against his well—your Kimathi was with him, and some other thugs, I don't know all their names—and presented me my terms of surrender: a few calming statements to Kirera's people, a move over to the government faction in Parliament, after a suitable interval, and—did you read any Shakespeare at secondary school?—'the rest is silence.'"

Ngano closed his eyes, and Okiri averted his own gaze. Outside the van, the lion had finally run out of patience. Rising to his feet and shaking his mane, the cat lumbered slowly toward the nearest car, planted his paws firmly in the dust, and began a low, steady growl. The tourist bus driver jammed into reverse and gave the animal a free path. Within a minute all the zebra vans had scattered off for other game, except for Ngano's.

Okiri tapped him on the shoulder, gently, as one would wake a child. The man's face was terribly thin, the cheeks drawn like those of a man who has kept his face always to the wind. "We'd better go, sir, we are alone again."

Ngano stirred. He fumbled with the ignition. It took several times to catch. On the horizon the other vans trailed dust and bounded over the ridges, running down warthogs in the late afternoon light.

OKIRI WENT TO his chief inspector and asked him for a few days off, muttering about a death in the family and looking sorrowful. Out of intention he had acted peculiar, but not suspicious, merely distant enough so that Kariuki might mumble something about "people from the lake" to his own tribesmen and write Okiri's behavior off as the strangeness of fellows who still plucked out their front teeth.

Before leaving for the coast, Okiri gathered some papers from his desk and his notebook and tossed them into an old East African Airways bag beside his shaving kit. Then, after a moment's reflection, he unlocked a bottom drawer and took out a hunting knife he had once received as a gift. It had an elegant sheath, tooled and branded in black and brown, and engraved on the blade was the picture of a building in San Antonio, Texas, called the Alamo. It was a gift from an American policeman who had come to Kenya on an exchange tour. In return, Okiri had given him a chrome-steel *panga*. The inspector threw the blade in among the files and zipped the bag shut. He signed out on the docket next to the door. He was on his own.

CHAPTER XIII

ELLEN REMEMBERED LITTLE of the ride down from the highlands. She had tried to sleep, wrapped in the tarpaulin. At first, the harshness of the road and the steady accumulating swirl of red dust that seeped in the back of the Land Rover kept her awake. With her hands tied behind her back, she could do nothing to wipe it away. But after some hours the roadway seemed to smooth to pavement and Ellen was able to rest, awakened only fitfully by the discomforts of her confinement: a pull on her shoulders as she tried to shift her weight, the burn of rope against her throat and wrists. From the front of the vehicle, submerged by the noise of the road and the rumble of the engine, came only faint swatches of song, short bursts of laughter, and then—as the night lengthened and her captors themselves became weary—silence.

The morning brought a gauze of light through the canvas and a sweet, humid heaviness to the air. Then the noise of the road vanished, the suspension began to roll and yaw, and as the breeze smelled of the sea, the Land Rover coasted to a halt in a soft wash of sand.

When they removed her blindfold she was in a small room, empty except for a cot, a chair, and a single table. On the table were a bottle of gin, a plastic tumbler, and a stack of *Country Life* magazines, two years old. Underneath the mattress was a chamber pot.

Through the barred window she could see a three-sided courtyard that was open to the sea. Sheltered under a cluster of coconut trees in the center of the courtyard was an old well. In the first hours of her imprisonment the man from the Land Rover—the short nun with the sneakers—sat on the edge of the well, peering back at her.

113

Once, while she turned momentarily toward the center of her room, he vanished and then reappeared at her door with a tray of food: a bright yellow omelette and a sectioned pineapple. Kimathi—she had heard the others call him that on the ride down from Kigeli—said the food was compliments of the Home Minister. He told her she was an official prisoner of the government. His voice intimated that she ought to consider it an honor.

"Then why aren't I in a police station?"

"Because you are a special prisoner. Material witness." Kimathi smiled, and after cutting the omelette into small pieces and offering her the plate and a spoon, he left the room. They were not going to leave her a knife.

Ellen spooned the egg to her lips. The awkwardness of the silverware made her feel like an infant feeding. She picked up a piece of the pineapple with her fingers; the juice of the fruit spilled down her lips. Since they had given her no napkin, she could only dab at the liquid on her chin with her hand. Already the stickiness clinging to her lips and fingertips in the humidity made her feel even more like a baby and reduced her pleasure in the sweet fruit. She wiped her hands on her skirt and, out of duty, continued to eat.

It all had to do with Jonathan, of course, and the strange story he had told her of Moguru's body. It was the only possible explanation. More people than he thought must be involved. Momentarily she regretted the advice she had given Grimes to go along with Bimji and carry out his orders.

Ellen sighed and lightly touched the base of her neck, the skin still raw where Kimathi had pulled the rope tight the night before. She could feel the thin streaks of scab that covered the lines where the skin had been broken. She had no mirror, but she could see flecks of dirt and dead skin come off on her fingertips as she brushed the wound. She ought to clean it, she decided, but they had given her no water. Her gaze searched the room's few objects, then settled on the gin bottle. Beefeater's. Skeptical, Ellen unscrewed the top and sniffed. It was real and not an improvised water jug.

Moistening a shirt sleeve with the liquor, she gently rubbed against the wound, the alcohol biting the skin as the juniper perfume swirled to her nostrils. For a moment, Ellen balanced her need for alertness against the tracing of fear in her belly and the heat of the sealed room, then she poured out an inch into the tumbler to drink.

114

She shivered slightly as the lukewarm liquid burned the back of her throat. Of course, she admitted to herself, they wanted her to drink. Why? To loosen her tongue? It would only be a matter of time before they discovered she really had nothing she could tell them. She knew the British were supposed to have done this to detained African leaders during the Emergency, hoping to break them and turn them out again, drunks, discredited in the eyes of their own people. It was part of Kenyatta's legend that he had refused them and, instead of drinking away the boredom, had taught himself Russian in the long years of detention.

They couldn't be crazy enough to intend to keep her here for years. And in whose eyes could she be discredited: Jonathan's, her students', her parents' in Weston, Massachusetts, dutifully filing clippings from *National Geographic*?

Ellen lay back on the narrow mattress. Balancing the drink on her sweat-dampened stomach, she closed her eyes—saw mountains—and blinked. There was the heavy air of the room, the dull metal of the cot frame, then eyes shut again, a blink: mountains. Each time she shut her eyes: the highland meadow, the mist, the mountain peak. She squeezed her lids closed, and into her consciousness swam the photograph. She had come to Africa because of a picture in a forgotten book: a black-and-white image of a highland farm, high in the temperate zone against the base of the mountain forest, heavy wheat in morning mist. It was the mist that drowned the edges of the picture and gave it that sense that mountain country sometimes has of having no connection with the lowlands: a darkened world, whole unto itself. There were no people in the photograph, and the farmhouse with its dark Tudor stripes was more English than African. But it was the strange shapes of trees in the distance and the jagged, unmistakable outline of the mountain peak that located the farm in a distant continent.

She had a sense that in such a country every view would be different from her home, a place unutterably distinct from the suburban reality in which she had been raised and schooled, a country with the cold vividness of a dream. The strength of that image had maintained her through the only way she had then known of getting from Boston to Africa—courtesy of the U.S. government. Somewhat shakily, she had managed to keep her austere vision through all the middle-class conviviality of Peace Corps training in a ramshackle vacation hotel in the Maryland mountains. By day African graduate students drummed Swahili into their skulls and by night, trainers and trainees, they all drank and put the make on each other while the married couples—depending on the security of their own ties—either participated or cheerfully watched.

One night, Ellen remembered, an abandoned house had burned down in a hollow near the hotel. The local volunteer fire company—one water truck and four retired coal miners—could do little but keep the flames from igniting the dry brush that backed up against the ancient Victorian frame. Everyone from the hotel and the neighboring town came down to watch the blaze, and the hill people seemed to give more distance to the Africans than to the fire itself: these strange black men and women whose skins were so much clearer and darker, whose bodies and bones were so much thinner and frailer, than those of the Negroes the Appalachian whites had known. The trainees—the white children, Ellen called them to herself—swelled with a condescending pride just to know these strangers whose faces, in the fire's gleam, shone forth with an alien elegance that the Americans had not seen in people of any color. But, that night, Ellen felt herself standing back from the others, sharing neither the spectacle nor the group delight. She simmered with impatience to get to Kenya, alone and on her own terms.

She had stayed on in Africa beyond the others, after they had packed their green trunks and returned to go to law school. The Peace Corps yoke had chafed her in direct, mundane ways: the meager allowance, the self-imposed austerity, the restrictions on having a car—an eight-thousand-mile-long lasso of *in loco parentis*. When her term was over she left the Peace Corps and arranged her own contract with the church school at Kongoru.

Now she was nestled up against the mountain in the photograph. The peak was visible every morning above her government-standard, cinder-block home. Most mornings. If it was not the time of rains. If she was not imprisoned in a whitewashed hothouse on a beach.

Ellen's mouth tasted of sour wool; the gin was a bad idea. She set her tumbler down on the floor beside her bed, walked to the closed door, and knocked sharply. She must have guards, if only Kimathi.

"Excuse me." She cleared her throat, addressing the blank door with a tea-party formality that seemed somehow appropriate to a disgruntled memsahib. "I should like a glass of water." Silence. "Would you be good enough to bring me a drink of water?"

There was a release of held breath—Ellen couldn't tell if it was her own or from out in the hall—then the door slowly moved in against her face. She stepped back to the center of the room. The open door let in a wave of cooler air from the shaded hallway. Standing inside the wave was a woman, chewing on a twig. She was smiling.

"They will bring your water, Miss Ferris. Please excuse me"— the woman latched the door behind her, and the breeze vanished— "I am the minister's wife. My name is Mukami."

She was one of the most beautiful women Ellen had ever seen, as beautiful as the mountain of the photograph. Ellen had realized soon after she came to Kenya that few of the women she saw could lay claim to that gleaming confidence that had so dazzled the Americans gathered on the Maryland hillside during her Peace Corps training. The market women trudging along the Kigeli roads, the farmer's wives hoeing in the fields, even the young girls crouching behind the desks in her classroom, were already beaten down, clothed in dull, flowered English dresses, the ill-fitting relics of the colonial obliteration of their culture, that they wore like a kind of penance. But this woman had none of that abnegation. She seemed inviolable.

Ellen stood in the center of the small cell as Mukami circled her, touching each object in the room as she passed. Fingers brushed the dust of the tabletop, tugged at the thin bedspread that covered the cot. Her eyes caught the tumbler on the floor, the broken seal on the liquor bottle. At the barred window she turned, and sat down on the cot.

"I'm curious about a woman who would involve herself in my husband's affairs. You must have been aware of the danger."

Ellen tightened. "I wasn't aware of any danger because I didn't do anything. I don't know why I'm here." As she spoke the door swung open again and Kimathi appeared, bearing a small tray.

"You must excuse us." Mukami waved a hand at the little man as if swatting a fly. "The freezer is broken. But the water should be cool anyway. Our well is deep."

As Ellen sipped the water, Kimathi leaned over and whispered something to his master's wife. Her expression darkened and Mukami stood erect. Without words, the two Africans left Ellen in the room alone, sealing the bronze lock behind them.

Ellen saw the woman twice more. Once she cried out in the night, shaking off a dream of fire, and Mukami was there beside the bed;

117

Ellen had not heard her enter. The faint light disguised the African woman, as if her skin were covered with a white powder, like the young boys Ellen had seen readying themselves for circumcision rites. Mukami reached a hand to Ellen's face, the long fingers growing in the night. Ellen flinched, but the hand merely rested on her forehead.

"You are sweating, Miss Ferris." The fingers lightly rubbed her skin. "Do you feel ill?"

Ellen tried to shake her head.

"A bad dream then?"

As the American woman started to speak, Mukami gently silenced her with a finger across the lips. "Don't talk. Sleep," she said, and Ellen was tugged back into a dreamless darkness.

When she opened her eyes—minutes, hours later—Mukami was gone from the bedside.

"Do you play gin rummy, Miss Ferris?"

The woman had moved—or left and then returned—and now she was sitting at the table, slowly dealing out solitaire with a pack of blue cards, in the full light of the morning.

Ellen straightened up in the bed. She realized by the dampness of her skin that she was still in her clothes, the blouse wrinkled, red dust lining the creases at the elbows.

"I'd prefer a bowl of water to wash myself." She ran a hand through the sweat-tangled mat of her hair.

"That can be arranged."

"Or a shower, a bath, something. Is there some way I can get clean?"

"Of course." Mukami continued flipping the cards as she spoke. She made no move to leave.

Ellen had slept well. But she didn't like the feeling that she had been watched in that sleep. She swung her legs to the floor and stood up. The energy of the morning erased some of her fear. "In America, Mrs. Mathenge . . ."

"I've lived in England."

"I'm sure. In America—and England, too—ladies who are lonely and very rich will hire young women to talk with them, to be companions. Did you bring me here to be a companion?"

"No."

"Because I don't want to be a companion."

"I didn't bring you here, Miss Ferris. My husband did." She gathered the cards together and placed them neatly at the corner

118

of the table. "I'm sorry if I've offended you. I was trying to be friendly."

"Tell your husband I want to talk with him."

Mukami began to smile. "Of course." Almost as an afterthought she added, "I can't guarantee he will speak with you."

"I didn't ask for a guarantee. I just feel I have a right to talk with him." Ellen paused a moment. Her next move was only perfunctory, but she made it anyway. "I don't like being treated as some kind of personal prisoner. I am a foreign national."

"You certainly are," Mukami said, and started to unlatch the door.

Ellen could see the long muscles of the woman's neck tensing as she adjusted the lock. Suddenly she called after Mukami, "Your playing cards," and reached out toward the pine table.

The African woman did not turn her head. "That's all right. They're for you. To pass the time."

The door slammed shut. After she heard Mukami's footsteps drift down the hallway, Ellen tried the lock herself. It was firm: a dead bolt on the outside of the door. She scanned the walls and ceiling for some kind of ventilation duct, but without hope. She knew from the soporific heat that the room had no outlet. She looked at the high window, and felt like shaking the bars, however pointlessly. But even beyond the bars there was a locked frame with grillwork.

"I won't let them make a monkey out of me," Ellen muttered to herself, then burst out into laughter, prolonging it long past the initial impulse, if only to draw comfort from the sound of her own voice rebounding in the closed damp chamber. As she laughed she could see Kimathi's sneakers through the crack underneath the door, drawing close.

Ellen picked up the deck of cards and kneeled on the floor by the door. "Tell Mrs. Mathenge I don't want to play," she shouted. Kimathi's shoes backtracked from the noise, and Ellen began to deal the cards one by one underneath the sealed door.

CHAPTER XIV

THE MINISTER'S COLLAR was too tight. He tried to insert a finger between the dark skin and the starch-tautened linen and could not. Mathenge grimaced into the mirror. He could feel the pulse of blood in his neck, the start of a headache. It was too damn hot.

The weather had been rotten. An unseasonable downpour in the night had thrown the normal balance of wind and water out of kilter, and now there was no cooling breeze from the ocean. The coconut palms hung limp. Sweat was starting to stain Mathenge's French cuffs.

In resignation he looked to the air conditioner in the window. The contraption was useless, its lurching, catarrhic hum lost in the steadier rush of noise from the surf outside. He turned the struggling machine off and threw open the window. A sore-mouthed yellow dog that was sleeping in the shadow leaped up at the noise, then slunk away, insulted. Mathenge could hear a clatter of dishes from the kitchen and the scraping of a chair from behind the barred window where they were keeping the American girl.

He should build a pool, he thought, looking at the courtyard's sun-burnished pavement. It would change the whole appearance of the place. He grumbled at the prospect of expense, though, especially when he didn't swim himself. Not that he hadn't tried. Mathenge had made an arrangement with the American ambassador to use his pool privately one afternoon a week. He had hired a Frenchman to instruct him, a handsome layabout who looked like something from a cigarette advertisement and who, as it turned out, could barely speak English. The Frenchman amazed Mathenge; he wore a different swimsuit each time. The minister certainly understood clothes, but he didn't understand the principle behind this—what was the Frenchman's point? Was he trying to coordinate with different shades of tan?

They tried a series of strokes together: first the Australian crawl, then, when Mathenge had difficulty breathing, a limping side-stroke. Mathenge ended up convinced he had some peculiar density, greater than other people's, which caused him to sink like a stone if he stopped moving for only a moment. He assured the Frenchman he did not have the same problem in salt water. His instructor agreed with him, but Mathenge soon discovered the Frenchman was the sort who would agree with anything he said. By the third session he noticed that the European had given up. He still gestured and puffed, miming strokes in the air and floating alongside the minister in the water like a concerned dolphin, but Mathenge knew the man had no interest in whether he learned how to swim or not. He was convinced Mathenge could never do it. So Mathenge stopped the whole business and, after some juggling of work permits, had the Frenchman deported.

Resigning himself to the heat, the minister put on his suit jacket, rubbed the shoulders smooth, sucked in his stomach, then relaxed. It did look good. He didn't have to suck in his stomach; that was the beauty of it. The tailor knew what he was doing. Mathenge smiled in the mirror, brilliant teeth, then heard a crash of china explode out of the kitchen. There was a high-pitched woman's laugh, the dog started barking, and a smoke of domestic havoc nosed through the open window.

"Stop it!" Mathenge shouted out the window. "Whatever it is, whoever is doing it, stop it! *Kwisha. Kabisa!*"

The trouble died to a twitter and then silence. Mathenge searched the room for his cigarette case, then saw the silver gleaming where he had left it on the windowsill. He must have been holding it a minute ago without knowing it. The minister walked to the sill, picked up the case, then quickly dropped it. It was burning hot. He kicked the case into the shade, waiting for it to cool, and licked the tips of his fingers. His grip was unsteady this morning, his nerves raw.

Mathenge looked back across the courtyard at the window with the iron bars. Kimathi bringing the woman to the coast, he decided, was a complete and irremediable mistake. Mathenge could not undo a kidnapping and return the teacher to her home with an apology from the government. They were now as much her hostages as she was theirs.

He tried to piece together Kimathi's reasoning. First of all, there

122

was Moguru—the Kigeli schoolteacher who was responsible for the Section's work in his district. It was his job to keep his eye on the local politics and oversee the group's poaching activities in the mountain forest. Moguru had twice failed to appear for important meetings. A quiet investigation had turned up nothing. Mathenge hoped it had been quiet—Kimathi was getting as loud as those insane bagpipe bands the army insisted on keeping active. The schoolteacher was now missing and presumed dead.

They had two suspects. The first was an American teacher at Moguru's school with whom the agent had openly quarreled. Kimathi didn't know what the teacher, Grimes, knew about Moguru's activities. But he was a drunk who talked to drunks, and that kind of network of loose tongues often knew a good deal. The second possibility was Bimji, a local merchant whom Moguru sometimes used as a conduit for skins and tusks. He seemed to do some work in the trade himself without—it had been assumed—any knowledge of the Section's involvement.

Unable to find Grimes, chased away from Bimji by some lunatic, and forced through his own bungling to shoot an associate of Bimji's, Kimathi had decided to hold the American's woman friend as a lever to get information from Grimes. But Kimathi didn't have Grimes and didn't seem to have much likelihood of finding him. He had disappeared as quickly and cleanly as Moguru. So now Grimes had no idea the woman was in danger. And Mathenge had in his charge an American citizen who might know nothing at all about Moguru's death.

Mathenge tested the cigarette case and withdrew an oval. He tapped it on his palm, lit it, and drew a long, puzzled breath.

Kimathi had simply enlarged the difficulties. He had, thought Mathenge, a country African's useless desire to please. He was the kind of boy who, if you asked for assistance, would give you wrong directions rather than admit he knew nothing. The minister crushed his cigarette. The trouble with such people was that you only found their limits after they had made a catastrophic error, never before. They were like pathetic cats who presented you with a dead bird as tribute and expected praise. But intentions counted for nothing in Mathenge's business. His usefulness to those in power around him depended upon a relative degree of circumspection. Dragging foreigners into the business was extremely dangerous.

Still, the woman might know something. Europeans were not innocents. Even if they had no money themselves, they knew about

123

money. It was, in a way, their birthright. They knew about buying and selling, about the great outside world where fortunes were made. They were not peasants or the sons of peasants. Their knowledge could be useful to men like himself.

"She is asking for you again, my husband."

Mathenge started at the voice, then saw his wife in the doorway. She leaned her head back with a slight tilt, looking at him with eyes at once amused and downcast, the way the old men and women might size up a goat in the marketplace. Unconsciously, he straightened his back.

Mukami poked a thorn-tree twig at her teeth while she waited for her husband's answer. It was a habit that had stayed with her since childhood, through Alliance High School, and through their time in England. The twig was a wand of independence for her, her magic against any attempt of Mathenge's to bully her or rein in her will. However closely she seemed to attend to what Mathenge said or did, the twig was always there, some portion of her mind always aloof, protected, utterly self-absorbed.

Mathenge spoke. "Is she frightened?"

"Not very. Kimathi comes in occasionally and makes silly threats. I don't think she's impressed. She treats him like a student."

"And you. How does she treat you?"

"She asks me questions. She doesn't tell me much. I don't tell her much."

"Does she know why she's here?"

"Do you, *mzee*?" Mukami used the honorific "old man." She ran her hand casually along the lapel of Mathenge's jacket, then swung it free. The square of brilliant yellow and brown *kanga* wrapped around her head caught a flash of sunlight. The smoothness of his wife's motions excited Mathenge, and the presence of her face in the light: the rising flare of her nostrils, the clean sculpture of the edge of her lips, the single glint of perspiration that fell across her cheeks from under the turban. He reached for her hand, but she ignored the gesture and walked toward the window. Mathenge dropped his fingers.

"Do you want me to let her go?" He spoke now only to her silhouette, her features obliterated in the windowlight.

"You can't let her go"—Mukami's voice was cold and disapproving—"but you should tell her that yourself. I don't like to carry your messages for you."

124

"I thought she might be more sympathetic to a woman."

"Perhaps, but not to me."

Mathenge snapped shut his cigarette case. "I'll go to her alone. Is anyone in with her now?"

"No. I think she's playing solitaire."

Mathenge grunted acknowledgment, then pulled down on the bottom of his vest. As he was about to walk through the door down the hallway, he turned to his wife one last time. "If you want to listen, I'll open the courtyard window. Is that satisfactory?"

Mukami nodded. She leaned against the window frame and gazed out toward the courtyard and the surf beyond, chewing silently on the thorn-tree twig, basking like a lioness in the warmth of the sun on her face.

AS MATHENGE SAT down in Ellen's room, he laid his cane across the table. He made a point of carrying it with him on such occasions: a strong shaft of ebony with a silver tip and a golden lion's head at the top. Other politicians might have fly whisks as symbolic echoes of tribal authority; Mathenge preferred something from London.

"Do you know Isaac Moguru?" he asked Ellen. There were no preliminaries. She stood in the center of the room, at attention. Mathenge surveyed her from the table, Kimathi from the bed. Unasked, the little man had moved through the door immediately after his superior and placed himself on the narrow cot, wiping the ticking clean of invisible dust before he sat.

"Yes, I've met him at conferences. He teaches secondary school in our district." She swallowed her breath. So it was Moguru.

"When did you last see him?"

Ellen's eyes were clear. "Three weeks ago," she said. There was a trace of hesitation in her voice.

"Did he seem healthy then?"

"Well enough."

"Did he say or do anything unusual?" Mathenge fingered the lion's head. Ellen noticed his smooth, manicured nails catching glints of the sunlight.

"He didn't say anything. His jaw was wired shut. I believe he broke it in a bar fight."

"With a friend of yours?"

"Yes." She rubbed the lines of soreness on her neck. "I was told

125

Mr. Moguru fell and hit his head on a spittoon. Is that the crime you are investigating?"

"Crime?" Mathenge turned in his chair. "Have we spoken of a crime?"

"Your associate here"—Ellen pointed toward Kimathi, who was dabbing sweat from his forehead with the heel of his palm—"told me I was under arrest as a material witness."

"You are under arrest." The minister eyed the small man with irritation. "But we are not concerned with a bar fight. We are investigating Mr. Moguru's murder, and we are interested in your friend. His name is Jonathan Grimes, isn't it?"

"Yes."

"Where is he now?"

"I don't know." Ellen tightened her hand into a fist. She was thinking, Bimji must have betrayed Jonathan. Or else Jonathan had somehow changed his mind, and Bimji had called the bluff about the schoolteacher's body. In either case their suspicion was on Jonathan now. They probably didn't even know about Bimji. Ellen's anger began to center on the heavy Asian with the hooded eyes who had dragged them into all this.

"We know he is not in his classes at school. That is derelict. We don't hire foreign teachers to run off on their own."

Ellen blinked. "My friend isn't the one you want," she said. "He didn't do it."

The minister's head tilted to one side. "What didn't he do?"

"He didn't kill Moguru."

"So Moguru is dead?"

"You just said he was murdered. You . . . the police"—she stuttered out the initial sound—"you must have the body."

"I said nothing about a body. I said we were investigating a possible murder."

"You did not. You said . . ." A trail into silence. She took her eyes from Mathenge's face and stared blankly at his cane lying on the table. There was nothing to be gained from arguing.

"You see, Miss Ferris, we often know more than we are aware of. You are a teacher. I am sure you see this every day in your classes. A good teacher can make students aware of hidden knowledge they don't know they have. They don't hide it out of malice, of course. They must merely learn to make the proper connections." The heavy skin around Mathenge's eyes creased into a smile.

Why is he talking so loud, Ellen thought, and answered herself:

126

he is trying to fill the space with his presence. Though part of her saw it as a ruse, she could feel another part responding, intimidated. A seed of confusion was planted. She no longer trusted all her reactions. She looked to Kimathi on the bed. The little man had his hands folded together on his lap and was staring at her, fascinated. He looked like a child at a magic show, a delighted, vacant expectancy in his eyes. She roused her resistance.

"How do I know your interest in all this is legitimate?"

Mathenge's grip loosened from the cane. He shaded his eyes from the windowshaft of sunlight.

"It is legitimate," he said.

"But the way you brought me here. You can't expect me to believe . . ."

"You mean the nuns?"

"Yes, I mean the nuns." Her voice snapped, explosive and bitter.

There was a pause in the room. Kimathi shifted on the mattress. The minister scratched the thick rolls of flesh on the back of his neck. He was embarrassed. It galled him to have to defend Kimathi's theatrics.

"It was necessary to do this quietly," he said, "for your sake as well as ours. You wouldn't have wanted us to haul you away in front of your students."

Ellen refused to look at his face. "I don't accept that. Not for a minute."

"You will have to accept it, Miss Ferris. It's not your place to judge us. You can give yourself any explanation you choose. If it makes you happy, you can say Moguru was my cousin and that is why I am concerned. Family and tribe—I believe that is what your sort believes is the engine of our government here. Very well then, Mr. Moguru was family."

Suddenly Kimathi spoke from his place beside the wall. "You know we have ways to make you talk, Miss Ferris, special ways." He started a smile, but in mid-grin a tremor of pain twisted his mouth. The minister had turned in his chair and smashed the small man in the side with the heavy end of his cane.

"Get out of here," Mathenge hissed. Kimathi clutched his ribs, a look of surprised innocence on his face. Without speaking, he scrambled off the cot and out the door to the hallway. Through the window from across the courtyard, a woman laughed, like a bird's cry.

Mathenge stood and retrieved his cane from the bed. "I am afraid we have nothing prepared for you so interesting as Mr. Kimathi's

127

fantasies," he said. "I have only one threat I can make. But it is a threat I would have no hesitation in carrying out." Slowly he sat back down in the plain chair. For a moment his gestures were weak, lifeless, as if the moment of anger at Kimathi had exhausted him. "I suggest it is best for you to accept that our interests and actions are legitimate. Otherwise, after finding what help you can be to us, we would have every reason to kill you, and no reason not to do so." He withdrew a handkerchief from the pocket of his suit jacket and dabbed at his palms. "Now, what else can you tell me about Isaac Moguru?"

Ellen made her decision. To be silent would be to sacrifice herself and throw Mathenge's suspicions on Jonathan. To tell the truth— if it were believed—would condemn only one man. It was a sacrifice she was prepared to make.

"The man you want is an Indian trader in Kigeli."

"Mr. Bimji?"

"You know him?" A touch of surprise edged Ellen's voice.

"We know of him, as we know of Mr. Grimes." Mathenge took from his pocket a small pad and a silver mechanical pencil, and Ellen told him the story Grimes had told her on the mountainside, only two days before.

When she was done, he drew a thin, careful circle on the page in front of him. "It was this Bimji who killed Isaac Moguru?" he asked.

"Yes."

"Why did he do it?"

"I don't know."

"How did he do it?"

"I'm not sure." Ellen saw Mathenge's pencil pausing in the air. She could feel his distrust, like a breeze. "I believe he was killed with my friend's kitchen knife."

"Your friend's? That is, Mr. Grimes's?"

"Yes."

"How do you know this?"

"Jonathan—Mr. Grimes—told me. May I have a drink of that water?" Ellen gestured toward the glass on the table. Mathenge nodded to her to take it and put his pencil down beside the pad.

"How do you know Mr. Grimes's story is true?"

"Because he wouldn't lie to me."

"How do you know that?"

Ellen sipped the tepid water from the tumbler. She swallowed hard. "Because he never has."

"That is enough for you?"

"Yes." The faintest of tears misted her vision. She studied the decaying plaster on the wall, then swung her view to the minister. Mathenge slowly raised his head. His face was heavy, obtuse, as if the features had been carved from some resistant stone. He matched the gaze from Ellen's eyes and then, with a gesture, broke it.

"This story of yours—or of Mr. Grimes's—you know it is difficult to believe. Mr. Grimes may have been lying to you. You may be lying to me to protect him. You are, after all, his whore."

The nails of Ellen's fingers dug into her palm. "That is not a term either Mr. Grimes or myself would use."

The minister's eyes hardened. "I will allow you your cultural differences, Miss Ferris. But please forgive me if I reserve judgment on the truth of what you say."

He rose to his feet, smoothed the fabric of his trousers, and leaned his weight against the black cane. "If what you say is true, Mr. Grimes and Mr. Bimji are both on their way to the coast. Is that correct?"

"That was the plan." Ellen had turned her back on Mathenge. She was staring out the barred window at the sun-dappled sea.

"Very well. I will send Mr. Kimathi to find Mr. Grimes and bring him here. Together we will arrange a reception for Mr. Bimji." Mathenge knocked on the door to be let out. After a moment of creaking metal, Kimathi, his face swollen with resentment, opened the latch from the passageway. The minister turned back toward Ellen, remembering his promise to his wife. "You understand, of course, that I cannot let you go until I have both your friends here."

"Mr. Bimji is not my friend."

"Once more your teacher's precision of language. Very well then, your friend and your enemy. And your enemy's money." He waited a moment for Kimathi to remove himself from his path. Then he nodded one final time at Ellen. "You are a missionary, isn't it?" As Ellen tried to speak he waved his hand in dismissal. "I know, this is another term you would not choose to use." He glared at the American and grasped the lion's head with both hands. "In any event, I suggest you pray that your Mr. Grimes was telling you the truth, that we can find him, and that he listens to reason. Please do that, Miss Ferris. It would be much better for all of us." The minister gave out the faintest release of breath, high and slight, like a baby's sigh, then shut the door behind him.

When she was left alone, Ellen's fear drained into an aimless jitteriness, as if she had drunk too many cups of coffee. Her tongue was dry; the skin of her cheeks burned. She felt flashes of anger at Grimes for getting her into this: valid, she decided, but pointless. She tried to drive the anger from her mind. She sat at the table, then rose in irritation, and leaned on the bed, leafing through the old magazines until her tense fingers tore the edge of a page. Suddenly, she threw the magazines down onto the cement and walked to the window. She reached up to clasp the bars and stared out past the well. When she saw what she had sensed would be there—Mukami's face, detached and still, an icon watching her endlessly in the heat—the pain in Ellen's head left her. Neither she nor Mukami made any effort to hide their gaze. Ellen felt oddly calmed, as if, their eyes firm on each other in the noonday, the two women were sharing some cup of dark, cool wine.

CHAPTER XV

GRIMES WINCED IN the sunlight, his head still heavy from Mfupi's banana gin. He kicked up a cloud of dust and watched it settle slowly on the line of gravel that edged the road, then lifted his eyes back out to the highway. His first ride had left him off outside of Voi: a German photo equipment salesman and his wife off to the western part of Tsavo where, on a clear day, you could see Kilimanjaro above the herds.

"*Mlima* means 'mountain' and *kilima* is a diminutive: 'little mountain' or 'hill,'" Grimes had told them while scrunched in the Karmann Ghia's back seat. "That's in Swahili. Now *njaro* also means 'mountain' in Chagga, or one of the other local languages there. So when you're saying 'Mt. Kilimanjaro'—which the missionaries probably made up—you're really saying 'Mount little-mountain mountain.'"

"Which is unnecessary?" said the wife.

"Right. Which is unnecessary."

She was doing the driving, swerving continually to dodge the mammoth chuckholes where the heat and rain had dug craters in the tarmac. These were left unfilled, the three of them decided, either to encourage freight to use the railway or as elephant traps to limit migration.

"So what can we call it?" the salesman asked, letting Grimes out as they turned off the main road.

He slung the pack over his shoulder and thought for a moment. "I don't know. No one would understand you if you used anything else."

"Ah, water over the bridge," said the salesman, nodding approvingly.

"Dam," Grimes amended.

The couple simultaneously lowered their eyes, taking offense at the correction. The woman slammed the accelerator to the floor. Grimes tried to wave and mime away the misunderstanding as the car lurched off into the heat, but they didn't look back.

For ninety minutes he stood there, and forty-seven cars passed him by. No one stopped. The line from the dust spun off the wheels of the passing cars moved up his pants legs from the shoes to the knees. He didn't use the American thumb-out move; he tried to wave the cars down with an extended arm and flapping palm. The thumb gesture had been the symbol of a banned opposition party, and the Kenyans probably had no sense of its hitchhiking meaning. It would have been equivalent, Grimes decided, to trying to get a ride in mid-Nebraska by standing along the highway waving the black flag of anarchy.

By midday there were more flies coming by than cars. The insects circled his head and settled on his eyebrows, drinking the beads of sweat caught in the damp hairs. Grimes used his flapping palm now mainly to sweep the bugs away. Finally he shrugged at the empty highway, squatted on the shoulder, and—with a momentary vision of his grandmother in his mind—tied a blue bandanna over his head to keep the insects off.

Grimes closed his eyes and pulled the loose cloth over his face. All he could hear was the wind swirling in an erosion gully behind his head and the buzz of flies landing on his shoulder. The sharp gravel pinched him through the worn jeans. He shifted his buttocks on the ground. Then low in the direction of the city he had left, he heard a truck's uncertain gear whine.

It rose out of a heat mirage: a bleating, squawking mobile barnyard dripping over the edges of a high, ancient pickup. The cab was a paste of green and brown paint and huge patches of rust, as if the feces of the chickens and goats in back had been conserved to coat the sides. In the rear the livestock were trapped in a cagework of rope and rough boughs: the wood knotty and untrimmed, the ropes slack and randomly tied like the web of a very old spider, the detritus of decades stuck to the strands.

The truck halted in front of Grimes, the left side of the vehicle swerving forward against an uneven brake. Two brown, curious faces peered from the cab. The driver had a trim mustache and a drooping forelock of straight black hair. It looked to Grimes as if the essential putty of Clark Gable's face had been pulled out at the cheeks, squashed and widened. His helper was younger, with a preternaturally straight nose and a fox's black eyes. Montgomery Clift in *Red River,* Grimes decided, a confusion of movies in his mind.

Clift waved a hand from across his friend's face. "Piss off!" he said cheerfully after a moment's scrutiny of Grimes. "You are not a woman."

Grimes untied the bandanna from his head. "No, sorry. I'm an American."

"We are Arabs," Clift shouted. He bared his teeth.

"No we're not." Gable looked reprovingly at his seatmate. "We're Pakistani." He turned off the ignition. The truck shook once, then sighed still. "Do you need a ride?"

"I'm going to Mombasa if you've got room."

Gable nodded. The driver released the hand brake and the truck started slowly rolling down the hill. "Piss off!" Clift sang again and opened the passenger door. After a second of puzzlement, Grimes grabbed his pack and hopped up the moving runningboard to the cab, then Gable lifted his foot off the clutch and the engine coughed into action.

When Grimes had stowed his bag between his feet and looked up again, the two men had sprouted twigs and leaves from their mouths. Clift was poking the sticks deep between his lips and stripping the leaves off with his teeth. Then he would toss the denuded twig out the window and replace it with a fresh leafy one out of a burlap sack that curled next to his side like a pet cat.

"Take some, please," said Gable, resting his palm against the windshield as a van passed them, spewing gravel behind its rear wheels. "It is *qat.*"

"For alertness," explained Clift, the pupils of his eyes swelling as he talked. He drew out a springy twig and waved it in Grimes's direction.

"No, thank you. I am a teacher."

Grimes coughed. He wasn't sure of the connection, but he felt his evening at Mfupi's had given him his fill of local intoxicants.

"Our religion has great respect for the teacher," Gable pronounced, swinging his head from side to side.

"Myself, I had a teacher once," Clift added. "He beat me with a stick, but he was very wise. He could count to ten in several languages." Meditatively, he chewed his cud. "He could do it very quickly, too. Very fast."

Grimes watched the rearview mirror on his side of the cab vibrate in the rush of road wind. The mirror was cracked down the middle, with a soiled strip of adhesive tape holding the two halves together in the frame. In it, he could see the plumes of dust the truck shot backward when its wheels slipped onto the shoulder and, between the sprays of dirt, a red Volkswagen beetle, wobbling back and forth across the adhesive tape. As Grimes watched, the Volkswagen gained on the truck, then suddenly faded back, allowing a Land Rover to pass both vehicles, before the beetle inched back up to the pickup's tail.

"But about engines, this one is the master." Clift clapped his hand on Gable's shoulder. "He taught me everything I know."

"But he knows nothing," Gable said, opening his mouth in wide laughter. He had no back teeth on top or bottom.

"This is not so." Clift fumbled in a heap of metal behind the cab seat. "Here, do you know what this is?" He waved the part in the American's face as if he were presenting Grimes a bouquet of flowers. Grimes studied it for a second.

"A head gasket?"

"Yes, yes, yes. A head gasket!" Clift tossed it back on the pile then kissed Grimes on both cheeks. "You are my brother," he said, and stuck some more leaves in his mouth. "This is not a fool," he said solemnly to Gable, pointing at Grimes with a twig.

Grimes's eyes went back to the mirror where the VW still drew forward and retreated, its image swelling and shrinking in a steady pulse, like a sea anemone filling with, and releasing, water.

"Do you know him?" Grimes asked.

"He is my best friend," said Clift and placed his hand on the driver's shoulder.

"I mean the man driving the car behind us."

The two truckers swung their heads around on the same pivot and peered down the sides of their vehicle. Quietly, Grimes rested his hand against the steering wheel.

"Piss off!" whistled Clift. "He is an African."

"But he has a white man's face," said Gable.

Jonathan strained to make out the image in the mirror. At a distance the face of the beetle's driver was ghostly, indistinct, a shade lighter than the neck beneath it.

"A stranger."

"No friend," agreed Gable.

Grimes gave control of the wheel back to the truck's driver. "Can you get away from him?" Grimes asked.

Gable's half-toothed mouth opened into its grin. "Hold on," he said. He downshifted quickly, then slammed the accelerator to the floor. Clift grabbed the door handle, getting set for the joyride, but nothing happened. The truck maintained its steady creep up the hill. Annoyed, Gable reached a hand through a hole in the dash and jiggled a rod. Suddenly the truck lurched forward, the goats gave tongue, and a dense, black puff of oily exhaust spumed from under the middle of the vehicle.

"At least we can obscure his vision," Grimes mumbled to himself.

"What, brother?"

"I said I hope he can't see us."

Clift nodded sagely. He lifted his hand to the side of his head and shouted some words in Arabic. Gable touched Grimes lightly on the shoulder. "He has asked Allah to strike him blind."

"A good move," Grimes muttered and began to slip slowly into the seat.

The beetle's high whine began to pull nearer the retching truck. Once the red car drew abreast of their cab, only to fall back behind the chickens and goats when the truck surged forward in a last burst of Gable's steam. In the instant the two vehicles were even, Grimes had gotten a clear look at the driver beneath him. He was a small African man wearing a khaki safari shirt and what seemed to be a Santa Claus mask. The rubbery flesh of the mask was nearly the same color as the shirt, the dull gray beginning to pick up the rosy tinge of too much road dust.

"He is a crazy man," Clift said, as the beetle again fell back behind the chattering livestock. The Pakistani's eyebrows were tense in the sunlight; bits of *qat* leaf stuck to his lips. He prodded Gable with his elbow to keep going, then turned his suspicious gaze to Grimes. "What does he want with you?"

Grimes threw his hands into the air in exaggerated dismay. "I don't know. I don't know him any more than you do."

Unbelieving, the Asian stared at Grimes. Then a sparkle of certainty flickered in Clift's eyes. His pupils shrank to laughing points. "I know," he said, starting to giggle. "Do not tell me anything. I know." He jabbed an elbow into Gable's side just as a thick geyser of spray and steam shot out from under the truck's rusting hood. A steady whistle like the opening squeal of an air-raid siren came from the straining engine, then a cascade of hot water flowed over the windshield. Gable slowed the truck down and grabbed a rag from behind the seat. Sticking his arm out the window, he tried to wipe a clear spot on the glass until a shot of the spray hit his fingers. With a howl of pain he dropped the rag and drew his scalded hand back into the cab.

"The windshield wipers do not," explained Clift with finality. "We must stop. Only temporary." While Gable eased the truck over to the shoulder, his assistant, with a *qat*-intensified coo, poured some drinking water from a battered jerry can over the driver's wounded paw. As they wheezed to a halt, the VW swerved by them, tried to brake, then sped on past, the expressionless, multicolor Santa staring out the window as he drove by.

"He is gone," cheered Clift, hopping around to the rear of the truck. "I know. Do not be afraid." He dragged another jerry can from underneath the goats and ran back to the engine. The water gurgled into the radiator, the hiss and steam gradually dying off to normality.

Clift raced back to where Grimes stood, anxiously peering off in the direction the red beetle had taken. The empty jerry can jangled against the truck driver's leg.

"Is it the sister or the wife?"

"You've got the wrong idea."

"I see. You are a quiet man about it. Very wise." Clift raised a shushing finger to his lips, but then sucked it with a slurpy laugh. "These African women," he said, "I think a husband is not enough for them." Grimes opened his mouth to speak, but Clift waved him off. "Don't tell me. I know. I am the man." He turned to Gable. "Aren't I the man?"

The driver swung his head noncommittally. He was trying to plaster bits of rag to the decrepit radiator. The engine was oozing a mess of fluids. Oil and water, mixing in filthy rainbows, seeped out of brittle gaskets and ancient metal, dripping to the thirsty ground. To Grimes it looked like nothing so much as the dying buffalo on the mountain near Landers's hut.

They had drawn near the coast now. The air was damp, the vegetation green on the low, brush-covered hills that ran off from the sides of the road. In place of the emptiness of the Tsavo plains there were now occasional signs of villages: small boys leading cattle over the hill paths, slat-board *dukas*—trader's shops—slumped into roadside gullies. The roadbed was narrower now, the sides steeper. Grimes began to feel trapped.

He jumped into the truck's cab to dig out his pack and brushed a hand over his shirt where Bimji's wallet was strapped. The movements caught Clift's eye.

"Where are you going, brother? This is temporary. Do you not believe? This man is a magician with the engine."

Grimes felt momentarily ashamed. "I'm sure he is"—he stuck his hand into an open, outside pocket of the bag—"I'm just getting something to eat"—and came up with a couple of tricorns of pastry stuffed with spiced potato: old *samosas* stained with cold grease.

"Want one?" He held out one of the crushed, greasy puffs to Clift. The Pakistani eyed it as if it were something fished out of a marsh.

"Where did you get that?"

"From a street vendor."

"When?"

Grimes studied the pastry. "Yesterday, I think"—Clift shook his head—"Maybe the day before."

"I will give you some of our food. It is more clean."

Grimes nibbled guiltily at a corner of the samosa as Clift began to sift through the rubber hose heap for wholesome food. The assistant was half-buried in the junk behind the cab seat and Gable was still applying tourniquets to the wounded motor when Grimes saw the red Volkswagen heading back at them from the direction of the sea. It seemed to bob and skid across the roadway, a rubber ball out of true, careering across his vision. Grimes tightened the straps on his pack and started to inch his way to the back of the truck as the beetle neared. The sound of his steps kicked off a frantic chorus from the animals. The odor of the chicken and goat excrement came over him in a single wave, adding nausea to his fear. He peered through the squawking fowl to where the beetle grew ever larger down the long, straight road, then looked behind him, to a cattle path that climbed into the brushland before losing itself in the low scrub. When the Volkswagen crossed the road and spun to a stop in front of the Pakistanis, Grimes started running up the eroded drainage ditch that stood between him and the rising cattle path.

He did not look back. He could hear a door slamming and footsteps, puzzled shouts from Clift and Gable, and then the firecracker pop of a pistol shot and the whine of a ricochet off the rocks beneath his feet. He dived off the path into the thick brush and spun around on his belly. He was sixty to seventy feet up the hill above the roadway. A bend in the path cut off the sight line from the shoulder where the beetle and truck were parked. Edging out underneath the branches, he saw the masked African motioning the truck drivers to the ground. Flat on his stomach, arms extended in the dust, Clift's face was turned toward the hill where the American lay watching. Grimes could see the Pakistani's eyes, huge black dots of shadow stamped by the sunlight.

The Santa Claus man yelled something at the drivers that Grimes could not hear, and they folded their faces into the dust. The African backed slowly toward the cattle path, his pistol still pointed at the prostrate men, then Grimes lost sight of him behind the overhang of the drainage gully. He was going to come up the hill. Grimes crawled back to the path, stumbled as a twig snapped in his face, and started to run again up the scrub-covered hill.

He had no idea where he was going. He wanted only to put more distance, and the curves of the cow path, between himself and the man with the mask. As he ran he felt a patch of wet warmth on his left cheek where the twig had cut his face. He brushed it with his fingers then felt a twinge of sharper pain as he pressed the flesh above the ring of bone that circled his eye. A thin path of blood edged his fingertips. Glancing at his footing, he grabbed the dusty bandanna from his back pocket and pressed it against the cut. The steepness of the hill dug into his breath.

There were no more shots. In quick turns backward, Grimes could not see the African. He heard him only as a scuffling on the hillside beneath him, a cascade of pebbles, the swing and snap of branches. The sound was not enough for the American to judge the distance between them. It contracted with each curve of the trail and each expansion of his fear.

At the top of a ridgeline there was a break in the brush. Before Grimes was a narrow ravine with a tangle of vines at the bottom, then, after one more lower hill, roadway again, and a cluster of shops. Men in white shirts slouched on the open grass before the *dukas.* The corrugated iron of the roofs reflected pink rays of slanting sun. The quick dusk was beginning.

Grimes tried to calm his frantic breath. I will be safe if I can get to the *dukas,* he thought. The only point of exposure would be going up the far side of the ravine. If he could stay under cover there, the man behind him would have to catch up on foot. At the stores he would not be able to risk wild shooting. Grimes knew the African in the mask was not a madman. He had sought him out on the road, and if Grimes was right, he had sought Landers out on the mountain.

Quickly Grimes descended the near side of the ravine, his heels digging and skidding in the soft earth as he slid down the cattle path. The bottom came abruptly, a jungle of nettles. A look back showed the African had not yet made it to the top of the ridgeline. Grimes pulled himself over the ravine bottom, fallen vines dragging at his feet, a moist mass of dead ferns sucking the tips of his shoes. Then he started his scramble up the far side of the ravine.

He was halfway up the far face when he saw the man in the Santa Claus mask come over the top of the hill behind him. He had flung the mask up to the top of his head and, silhouetted against the setting sun, seemed to have sprouted a grotesque tumor on his skull. Grimes watched the gunman pause in front of the sky and brace the pistol in his hands, swinging in a slow semicircle, scanning the ravine. Grimes rolled into the bushes at the path side, still hidden beneath the steadily rising shadow line cast by the dying sun over the hillside. Perplexed, the African dropped his pistol to his side and stepped uncertainly down the ravine.

As long as the man was on the steep slope Grimes knew he would have no footing from which to try an accurate shot. In the pause, Grimes made a run for the top, up and over the edge of the ravine. It took fifteen seconds to make it over. He knew because he counted them out loud to drive the fear from his mind. One one thousand. It brought back the crazily inappropriate memory of playing tag as a child. Two one thousand. The cool spring air blowing through the fence of a school playground. And then he was over the top, blocked again from the gunman, looking down at the roadway and the cluster of country shops.

Grimes descended the gentler path, stopped, and crossed the road. The sun had almost completed its sudden evening drop. A cool of night rose from the ground. The men at the shops had retreated under the corrugated iron canopies. Their backs toward Grimes, they leaned forward over the counters of the *dukas,* waiting for a box of matches, a bar of soap. Only a young girl behind one of the counters could see the American as she passed a handful of cigarettes to a customer. She noted his appearance with a slight turn of dark eyes, but said nothing.

Grimes approached the largest of the low buildings and stepped into a barroom's sudden darkness. In the long shed were perhaps twenty men, clustered around four tables and spread along the homemade wooden stools that lined the bar. The heads of what seemed a forest of half-driven nails caught the yellow light of a kerosene lamp that stood on the far edge of the counter. The bits of metal shone at the joints of the plain wood braces that supported the stools, and gleamed along the planks of the wall.

Stares acknowledged Grimes's entrance, nothing more. He took a seat at the bar next to a large man in a red shirt. The drinker's hair was clipped close to the skull and Grimes could see cords of muscle at his neck that ran in a solid line down his arm and around a brown bottle of beer. Grimes nodded briefly to the man, eyed the door, and sat down. A gray-haired barman, in a white undershirt that smelled of starch, glided over to Grimes.

"What do you want?"

Grimes brushed a hand by the corner of his eye. The tip of his forefinger was coated with the red glimmer of the African dust and the drying of his own blood.

"A beer. Tusker."

"Warm or cold?"

"*Baridi sana.* Very cold."

The bar man gave a Kenyan assent, shaking his head as if there were something stuck to the top of it that he wanted to get off. He reached to the back wall and pulled a Tusker from the bottles floating and clanking at the bottom of a styrofoam picnic box. On the side of the box was a half-done, abandoned painting of the Kenyan flag. Prying off the cap, the barman handed the bottle to Grimes.

He tipped it to his mouth and swallowed a rush of bubbles, warm as shaving soap. It was not *baridi sana*. The beer was the same temperature as the close air of the bar, the bottle only a little clammier from its bath in the cooler.

Grimes's fiddling with the tepid Tusker had caught the attention of his neighbor in the red shirt. He could feel the man's eyes studying him.

"It's good," the man said in English and started to swing his head slowly from side to side.

"Yes it is." Grimes smiled and lifted the bottle in imitation of the newspaper advertisements.

"Very good, very very good." The African's head was still swinging. Both of the big man's thick hands were now clutched around his own beer bottle.

140

Grimes was sure the man was drunk. He was not sure he was happy. With the masked man outside somewhere looking for him, Grimes did not want anyone to be unhappy with him inside the bar. With a wave of his hand, he called the barman to bring another Tusker for the man in the red shirt. The bar door opened just as the top was lifted off the new lager.

The gunman no longer had the pistol in his hand, but Grimes had no trouble recognizing his gait. He wore a heavy cover of red dust over a shabby suit jacket. His features were puzzled, earnest; his nose, permanently wrinkled, as if it had been broken and badly set. Here among the other men, without a weapon, the man appeared slighter than Grimes had imagined him out in the ravine. He found Grimes's eyes quickly, looking at the American as if he had done him some irremediable injury.

The little man walked to the empty stool closest to Grimes, just the other side of the man in the red shirt. He swung the cloth of his jacket clear of the seat before sitting. Grimes could see that the garment was not shabby as he had thought, but simply too big, the hand-me-down of someone more substantial. Its right-hand pocket sagged as the man sat down. Without moving his head, he gently patted it, testing, then ordered a beer in a broken, upcountry Swahili that marked him as a stranger to the fluent local men. His eyes no longer acknowledged Grimes.

In the momentary truce, the American considered his options. A run for the door would be foolish, suicidal. Even if he could make it outside into the night, the gunman would be no more than a few steps behind. The running itself might be construed by the men in the bar as an admission of some kind of guilt. Grimes remembered shopkeepers in Kigeli charging into the street at one man's cry of "Thief! Thief!" and running a teenage boy to the pavement, sticks whistling through the air. There would not be an opportunity for explanations.

If he stayed in the bar, he might be safe, but sometime he would have to leave. The man in the red shirt, still contentedly swaying his head, offered Grimes his only chance. Slowly he reached his foot out into the stool legs of the man seated next to him. Gently, he lifted. There was a faint creak of wood and then the red-shirted local, his head already swaying with beer, began to lean into the sullen gunman like a listing ship, his world tipping over.

The drunken man reached out and grabbed the gunman's shirt

to steady himself. The smaller man pulled away from the wave of alcoholic breath, but the man in the red shirt would not let go. While Grimes watched, both men teetered on their stools. Grimes flicked his foot a second time, and the two Africans crashed to the floor.

"You are a drunken fool," the little man said, propping himself up on one elbow.

"Fool?" said the man in the red shirt—his eyes looking about at the other men in the bar as he tried to regain sufficient sobriety to let himself be insulted—"Who you calling fool, fool?"—and reached to yank the little man's arm out from under him. The outsider's shoulder thudded to the concrete floor.

There was a sound, half yowl, half growl, and suddenly the gunman's movements sped up in a flush of adrenaline and irritation. In the same swift motion he spun over, clamped a hand on the drunk's wrist, and reached down into his jacket pocket for the pistol.

He had no time to use it. At the first glint of metal, a foot in a black plastic shoe crushed the small man's hand and gun into his kidney. Two men from the nearest table jumped on him, prostrate on the floor, as if they were leaping into a pool. The man in the red shirt, straining with his free arm, grunted something unintelligible at Grimes and mimed a loose, stabbing motion in the air. Grimes handed him an empty Tusker bottle down from the bar. The drunk's blow with the bottle missed the gunman's head by an inch; the fragments of flying glass hit everybody else. When Grimes left the bar the man in the red shirt was not much better off than his enemy. The first two combatants were the center of a pile of fists, boots, and bodies: a field of ants swarming to sweetness.

Grimes left some coins on the counter and walked quietly out the bar door, leaving the tumult and kerosene light behind. The night was fresh now. The starlight had filtered away the dampness. He spotted the gunman's mask by the roadway, propped up in the grass, and bent to pick it up. The rubber had been torn across the beard and nose. Grimes folded it as neatly as he could and stuffed it into the pocket of his jeans: a memento of his triumph.

He took a step down the road and turned east toward the sea. For a moment he warmed himself by the lights of Mombasa, close over the hills. The sweet, pale light refreshed him, a memory of day. Then he heard again the sound of engines behind him and saw the flare of headlights around the curve. Grimes turned. He knew of a shelter in Mombasa. The mask stuck in his pocket, whistling the "Marines' Hymn," Grimes stepped into the light to flag down one more ride.

CHAPTER XVI

GRIMES HAD NEVER been stung by a bee before he came to Africa. It was a matter of some concern to him. One of the earliest memories he had of his father was of the man sent to bed by a flurry of bee stings at a softball game, the skin of his cheeks red and swollen by his irritated body chemistry until he looked like one of the drunken, blundering British colonels that lingered in the corners of Nairobi bars, bragging and mourning their past.

Despite his worries about anaphylactic shock, Grimes had never fled from bees at home, but merely watched them circle blossoms, with a dreadful wariness, too proud of his adolescent dignity to run. In Africa, the air swarming with every kind of insect, he had perfected the show of stoicism that coated his inner fear and curiosity like the thinnest of pastry shells. When the first irritated bee settled on his forearm as he rode in a Land Rover taxi down a red Kigeli road, time stopped for him. He watched, frozen, as the insect tottered on the sunburned hairs of his arm, arched its striped body in suicidal pleasure, and plunged the sting into Grimes's flesh. Only after the action was irrevocable did he sweep the bee away.

The sting was nothing, a bit worse than a bad mosquito bite. There was no allergic reaction. Grimes was ecstatic, a huge inherited weight lifted from his shoulders. Somewhat idiotically he showed his minor wound to the other passengers in the taxi. They were polite, but unimpressed. But their lack of enthusiasm did nothing to dim his own buoyant relief, a feeling of invulnerability that lasted until the next time he stepped into a procession of fire ants.

It was with that same psychic relief that Grimes walked under the sheet-metal elephant tusks in downtown Mombasa, an hour after his escape from the gunman. For the first time since his run from Bimji's refrigerator, he felt he was leading the game against enemies who, with the appearance of the man in the Volkswagen, were no longer unseen.

His hitchhiking fruitless, a local bus had taken him from the bar into town: one of those vehicles that materialize in the hazy accumulation of shanties and warehouses that mark the outskirts of an African city. Leaning over the backpack on his lap, he had napped fitfully until the regular line of the city's streetlamps flashing by awakened him. In the new light he had seen the fleeting image of Clift and Gable hunched over the truck's innards in a mechanic's lot, the animals in the back squalling in the thick, sea-laden air. The gunman had not gone back for the truck drivers; a load of guilt lifted from Grimes's mind. He felt happy in the night, happy and hungry.

At a small residential street, he turned off the promenade of Kilindini Road. Entering a soft, pastel row of comfortable stucco flats, he knocked on the one front door he knew in Mombasa. The building was a bright pink, dimmed by the evening. In front of the barred windows were four tiny plats of failing grass, each no larger than a grave marker. Out of the dirt of the side alley grew a palm tree that wore a sash of barbed wire around its trunk. From a window to the left of the main door an air conditioner dripped water over the greenest edge of one of the tiny lawns.

Struggling against the air conditioner, Grimes's knocks brought no answer until, scanning the entrance, he twisted an ornate key that protruded out of the door frame. An overly loud electronic chime rang out four notes that seemed to have nothing to do with each other.

From inside the house came the slam of a door and a shout in garbled Swahili. The main door opened, and a man with wire-rim glasses perched around the hard, enormous temples of a skeletal face stood staring at Grimes. Clutched in his right hand was a dishcloth.

"So who are you?"

"Grimes, Mr. Berryman. Jonathan Grimes." He swung his backpack down to the sidewalk. "I came down here with a Scout troop last year."

There was still no sign of recognition from the older man.

"You let us use your church and schoolyard. I thought . . ."

At the word "church," the hard face softened, and smiled.

"Of course. Grimes. You came down with a local fellow. Nice bunch of boys, I remember them now. Polite. Hardly said a word." Berryman glanced down at his fingers, stuck the dishcloth in his pocket, and reached out to shake Grimes's hand. "Well, come on in. You'll be wanting dinner, I presume. Everybody wants dinner."

The missionary grabbed Grimes's pack and slung it over his own shoulder. "Ma, there's an American here. Put on another plate," he shouted to an indistinct kitchen and led Grimes into a central parlor.

Grimes's first sense of the room was that it was incredibly small and cramped, but he soon realized that this was an illusion. It was simply the living room of a Midwestern tract house—slightly over-stuffed and soft—surrounded by a moat of completely empty space. Every piece of furniture—the brown suede divan, the drop-leaf veneer table, the bronze lamps with ruffled shades—was at least ten feet from the nearest wall.

Berryman noticed the puzzlement on Grimes's face. "We've been robbed," he said. He steered Grimes to one of the wide windows that looked out onto the side alley and the sickly palm. "I'm not sure how they do it, but I think they use hooks and poles, kind of like fishing. They can break a pane down here, even through the grillwork, and then mosey the pole right into the room and snatch what they want."

"You've seen somebody do this?"

"No. But it makes sense to me. Nobody's pole can be that long, so the stuff's safe in here." He shook his head. "There are a lot of sorry thieves out there."

Berryman plumped one of the pillows on the sofa and pointed for Grimes to sit. Behind his wire-rims, Berryman's glance spun around the room. "I said we'll need another chop, Mother," he shouted, then turned to Grimes with an apologetic shrug. "The woman can't hear."

The two men stood silently for a minute while Berryman nervously paced the imaginary borders of his inner living room. Grim, irritated lines grew around his mouth. He looked to Grimes like a surgeon waiting for a disorganized nurse to find the proper instrument.

Suddenly Mrs. Berryman walked in with a piece of raw meat in one hand and a bag of Cheese Whizzes in the other. She was a strong, square woman, not taller than her husband, but more monumental, bulkier, all muscle. Her face was sullen, a sheet of straight lines.

"Here's your meat, Luther. Just watch your meat," she said.

Berryman nodded, and the woman returned to the kitchen. He adjusted a shortwave that sat on the edge of the dining table and an Armed Forces Radio rebroadcast of an Orioles-Yankees game crackled on. "Come out here and help, son," he said to Grimes and led him across the no-man's-land of empty space, through a sliding door with movable grillwork pulled back, and out onto a narrow balcony. "Just like home," he said proudly, and hunching over a tiny barbecue grill resting on a wooden stool, began to blow on a bank of coals. The white edges flared to flame and cast an odd, dancing hell-glow over the smooth curve of the missionary's glasses and his ballooning cheeks.

Grimes shivered; the sight unnerved him. "The light's strange," he said, searching for words. "It makes you look like a cross between the devil and . . . Dizzy Gillespie."

The air drained from Berryman's cheeks. He straightened up, puzzled distaste on his face. "Who?"

"He's a jazz trumpet player. Dizzy Gillespie, that is."

"I wouldn't know anything about jazz."

"Well, he puffs his cheeks like that when he plays." Grimes trailed off. He wanted to celebrate his victory at the bar, but there was no way he could even begin to confide his difficulties to a man for whom Dizzy Gillespie, jazz, and the devil all seemed equally suspect. He rested his hands against the Asian's money belt, more alone than ever.

As the meat seared on the grill, Mrs. Berryman continued her steady trek between the kitchen and the compressed living room, piling soft food on the table: cottage cheese, turnips mashed in cream, candied carrots, like the shiny slices of a souvenir dwarf tree trunk, glossed for sale. The strange American smells mixed in the air.

"Sometimes I wish, Jonathan, that the black people would go away"—Berryman speared a chop off the grill—"I hope you don't mind my saying that. I don't mean it seriously, of course. It would defeat my purpose in being here, no one to shepherd after all. But as an American, I'm sure you can understand the frustration."

"Don't say such things, Luther." Mrs. Berryman frowned across the table. Given the hardness of her face, her voice was surprising:

accommodating and soft. As they exchanged pleasantries and the pork chop, sudden smooth flashes crossed her stern features, grandmotherly smiles that appeared and disappeared like glimpses of unexpected terrain in bursts of lightning. The changes of expression spooked Grimes. They were disturbing, unexplained by anything being said.

"I don't think I quite understand you."

"It's the thievery, the deceit. I have to chain the chairs to the floor of the church or they'd take those. And half, more than half, of the students in the primary school are Muslim. They have no intention of becoming like us. There's resistance at every turn." A suspicion crossed his face. "But then you're not really a Christian yourself, are you?"

"My school's Methodist."

"But yourself. You're merely a teacher. You prepare your students for examinations. That's your goal." A beatific grin returned to his features. "Is that unfair?"

"It's not unfair to me. It might be unfair to the students. They want an education."

"That's it exactly." Berryman piled more of the half-done chops on a blue china plate and took them back to the table, pausing to seal the balcony door behind him with a series of padlocks fit for a sea chest. "They'll pick a church on the basis of the school it runs. What kind of Christianity is that? The government encourages it. I prefer the older people, even with their ignorance. They have no hypocrisy. Ah, this is perfect." The missionary cut into his chop, relishing the bright pink meat.

"Aren't you afraid of trichinosis?" Grimes asked.

"I'm not afraid of anything that's got to do with my stomach," Berryman replied. "I can take anything Ma can dish out."

Grimes had come here for the food, the tastes of home, Mrs. Berryman's pantry lined with Betty Crockerisms. It was to be his reward for the escape on the road from Nairobi. He had remembered the kitchen ever since Moguru and he had taken the Scouts to the seacoast. The students had shared the maize and beans of Berryman's parishioners while Moguru and he had dined at this table—turkey and cranberry sauce—Grimes savoring the delicious alien bird. But now the food was making him queasy, whether it was the bland, soft vegetables themselves, or the memory of the man chasing him down the highway in the world outside the missionary's charmed, compressed enclave.

Berryman's appetite, however, was immense. The bony man stuffed himself, emptying serving dishes that his wife, with a phlegmatic efficiency, was somehow always able to refill. She seemed to gain a satisfaction in rendering her husband's consumption useless, until there was more food on the table at the end of the meal than at the beginning.

"The problem is we're still foreigners. I've lived here thirty years, and they treat me like a stranger. They're polite all right, but it's the politeness you'd show a stranger. So when you speak of sin, of salvation, of redemption—of the things that count in this world—they ignore you. Blind incomprehension, if not hostility. They're like savages. I know I'm not supposed to say that. But I'm not saying they are savages. That's not the point. I'm saying they're *like* savages. They've got no understanding in their hearts."

"Maybe you and they have got different expectations."

"You bet we've got different expectations!" Berryman's last forkful of creamed corn nearly exploded from his mouth. He sputtered and dabbed with the soft, white napkin. "Did I ever tell you about myself, son, my own background?"

"No, sir, you didn't."

"I don't suppose I would have. With that other fellow along." Berryman grew silent for a moment, adjusting the silverware at the edge of his plate. In his mind, Grimes saw again the earlier visit: Moguru and Berryman, full of scornful politeness, trying with what each one presumed was mandarin cunning to veil his own assurance of superiority.

"Well, I'll tell you what I expect. I expect revelation." Berryman banged his fist on the table, scattering the dessert spoons he had just toyed with. "I received—and understood—the word of God, forty-five years ago, in a boxcar on a railroad siding in Kankakee, Illinois. And I expect nothing less for these people."

"Kankakee?"

"Illinois Central line. Forty-five years ago last month." A grim, storytelling determination shone from Berryman's face. His wife began to rub her brow.

"I had run away from home, following the freight lines all over the country. Beautiful places. I went down south just when the new grass was coming up. They were weeks ahead of my own home and the nights were already warm, and that grass was the brightest, shiniest green you've ever seen. And then I humped the

150

Great Divide to Grand Junction and saw the mountains—the real mountains—for the first time in my life.

"But I didn't have any money. I was big and strong but I wasn't interested in working. I became a thief. I stole money. I stole food. I stole chickens and apples and a pair of blue trousers and a cream-colored Stetson hat. I stole more than I needed, and I gambled away the rest riding along the prairies, drinking rotgut whisky, until I couldn't tell the ace of spades from the queen of hearts. Fornication, blasphemy, scorn. You name it, and I did it. Seventeen years old. I could barely shave my face. I'm not proud of this, son, I'm just bearing witness. When I talk about having a savage heart, I'm not casting stones at anyone. I know what these people feel like."

"Which people?" Grimes shifted, uneasy in his chair. "Do you mean kids, or evil people, or the people here in Mombasa?"

Mrs. Berryman sealed her heavy hand over Grimes's. "Don't interrupt when Luther's talking."

"It's all right, Mother, you can just leave him alone." The missionary put both hands palm down on the table and stared at Grimes. "When I say 'these people,' son, I mean everybody. You and me and Ma and the blacks, too. They're not special. I mean everybody."

"So what happened in Kankakee?"

"In Kankakee I was saved." A huge, static-torn cheer came out of the radio, a final out. As someone started talking about razors and skin, Berryman clicked the set off. "It was night, son. I'd crawled into an empty car on a siding to sleep it all off. I slid the door shut with my foot and pillowed myself on my coat as best I could. I must have been asleep some hours when I heard a clanking outside the door. I knew it might be a bull, so I tried to melt into the corner and not make a sound, not a breath. But no one came inside. Just more clanking and the sound of a hammer, three times, ringing like a bell. Then I heard this voice, someone leaning right against the side of the car, right next to me, a deep man's voice, the wood vibrating with each word he spoke.

"It was one of the guards, a big black man, we all knew him. He told me I was going to stay in that boxcar awhile, until I changed my mind about things. He said he knew me and that he'd let me out just as soon as I gave him to know that I wasn't going to keep on doing the things I'd been doing. He said I could scream and yell all I wanted, but he'd be the only one who could hear me. He told me I was going to be a better person or I was going to starve."

"It's a hundred percent true," said Mrs. Berryman, who was passing slices of apple pie around the table from an aluminum tin, smothering each with a soft, melting ice cream. "It was up to him."

"You didn't think he was just trying to scare you?"

Berryman raised his chin; his mouth was small and round. "No, why should I think that? He could have just left me there. No one was going to miss me. No one cares about one more dead bum."

Grimes persisted. "But someone would have heard you."

Berryman shook his head. "You're missing the point, son. Nobody heard. I tried. I yelled and screamed but nobody came back. Just that black man. He'd come and tell me I wasn't ready yet. Two days went by. I could see the light come and go, pouring through the boards. I got hungry, and I got tired. And all I could do was listen to the sounds of the trains and that black man coming by to the side of the car every couple of hours, whispering right against the boards: 'Are you ready yet, son? Are you ready?'"

Without taking his gaze from Grimes, Berryman accepted a plate of the pie and began to spoon it to his lips. "Then on the third night, when he came back, I was ready. It was just like that." The missionary snapped his fingers in front of Grimes's eyes. "I heard the ringing of that hammer on the bar, and then the black man slid back the door and embraced me and told me I was saved. And I was. Of course, I had to go to jail for thirty days. But after that I became the man I am today."

"Did you go back to your family?"

"No. Why should I do that? They were no more holy than anyone else. I went out to spread the word of God. I studied some. I married Ma, and we came out here." Berryman licked his spoon clean and rested it on the tiny plate.

Grimes couldn't eat anymore; the missionary's story had unnerved him. He felt he had missed something, that he was being tricked.

"But why Africa? Why here?"

"Because there is a whole nation here just like I was before that man set me free. And I mean to save them, every last savage-hearted one of them."

The three Americans sat silently around the table. The air tasted sour to Grimes, the way it had as a child when a family fight had been finished, but not settled. He spoke with difficulty.

152

"I don't think you can expect that of people. You can't put them through your own personal history just because you've got some schoolbooks or a church building. That's not fair to them."

"No one's talking about fair, son. We're talking about God. I'm saving these wretches from eternal death. What are you doing for them? Teaching them how to spell?" Berryman was sneering, the ice cream glistening on his lips.

"I teach history," Grimes said, his voice dropping to a whisper.

"History!" Berryman reared in his seat. "Why?"

"So they'll pass the East Africa Certificate Examination and maybe get a job. I do what they ask me to do."

"That doesn't speak much for your moral independence."

He doesn't know the half of it, thought Grimes, but he said, "I'm a guest in their country. They know their own needs better than I do."

"Oh my, my. Their own 'needs.' You sound just like our home missionary board. A bureaubrat in the making. Their own needs." Berryman chuckled, then stopped abruptly. His voice exploded across the table. "How long have you been here?"

"Two years."

"Two years! How in the name of God do you presume to let these children tell you their needs? Haven't you seen them? Haven't you looked into their eyes? There's nothing there. They've got minds as empty as an unplowed field. You haven't seen a thing, son. Nothing."

Grimes grabbed at Berryman's words, fumbling for a reply. His face was glowing in the humidity, his temples pounding. "A couple of minutes ago you told me they were all thieves. Now they're all children. Just which the hell is it?"

"Children can be thieves, son. You haven't heard a word I've been saying. You weren't listening to my story."

"He shouldn't swear." Mrs. Berryman spoke, wrath in her eyes, her heavy head shaking. Grimes watched her husband's long, bony fingers patting her hand in comfort.

Grimes rose from his place at the small, cramped table. Coming to this house was worse than whatever was waiting outside. Around him clustered the huddle of American furniture and the *cordon sanitaire* of empty floorboards beyond. "I'm sorry," he said. "I've got to go now. You'll have to excuse me."

The missionary's wife stolidly scanned the table. "But you haven't eaten your dessert." Her words were more a judgment than

153

a complaint. Berryman wiped the mist of humidity from his spectacles.

"I thought you were going to spend the night."

"I really can't afford to," Grimes said and started to gather his things together.

"Suit yourself," Berryman shrugged, "but don't forget to thank Ma for the dinner."

"I wasn't going to forget." Grimes tried to veil the irritation in his voice. He turned toward the woman who was scraping leftovers together onto a bone-white platter. "It was a fine home-cooked meal, ma'am. I thank you."

Mrs. Berryman nodded and kept scraping.

I have got to get out of here, Grimes thought. As he threw the backpack over his shoulder his fingers were trembling. Shifting his feet he waited while Berryman slowly undid the two massive bronze locks on the front door. The missionary waited an instant until Grimes stepped outside, then slammed the door shut, the two latches reverberating in the hot night like piano wires obliquely struck.

The warm city air weighed on Grimes's lungs. He felt out of breath, then realized his heart was still racing. I can't handle Americans anymore, he thought to himself. I've lost the touch. I've lost my natural immunity.

He hurried out of the quiet of the stucco houses, back to Kilindini Road. The hotels and restaurants were still open; tourists and locals wandered into the dining rooms open to the night. A smell of lobster and drying fish came from doorways and mixed with the odor of grilled corn from the *jikos* of sidewalk vendors. The food smells did nothing to lessen the oppressive weight of the air on Grimes. He had to get out of the city. He counted the remaining notes of his own money—leaving Bimji's sealed in the wallet around his waist—and hailed a cab.

The taxi dropped him off over the Nyali Bridge at the start of the North Coast Road. His own money gone now, he would hitch once more the last leg to the rendezvous with Bimji on the beach. He could hear the sea, but not see it; the steady, soft fall of the breakers hidden just behind the rows of palms that shaded the road from the moonlight. For a moment he was hypnotized by the white sound, until the flare of yellow headlights broke into his trance, the two beams bouncing along the uneven surface of the road. Grimes stepped into the glow and waved his palm. The car pulled

154

up, changing in the near light from gray to red. A small African man, his face a mass of bruises, lifted a pistol from beneath the dash and motioned to the American to open the door. Exhausted, Grimes stepped into the car.

CHAPTER XVII

IT WAS THE night porter from the Mombasa train who sent Okiri to the harbor. He had remembered Bimji as the sullen Asian with the little girl who had broken down his own compartment door. When the employee had pleaded with Bimji to report the damage to the station office, the Indian had said nothing and walked away.

The porter had been worried he would get blamed for the trouble and had his cousin, a taxi driver, follow Bimji and the girl, until he lost the pair in a crowd near the Dhow Wharf. That was where the inspector caught up with them, opposite Fort Jesus.

They were walking hand in hand along the road that led from the former Portuguese guardpost into Old Town. Okiri saw them cross the single sharp line of dark that separated the coastal sunlight from shadows, and then they were gone. Hurriedly the inspector brought the Capri over into the car park of the fortress, stuck a hand-scrawled sign that said "POLICE" in the window, and, dodging the afternoon traffic, ran over to the warren of narrow streets that made up Mombasa's old quarter.

The tall, shuttered houses blocked out both the sun and the sea wind, making the sidewalks narrow inlets of a stillness that was darker and damper than the surrounding avenues. Okiri pressed his way through the crowd of shoppers, trying to keep his eyes fixed on Bimji and the girl. He could see the Asian's head, halfway down the block, bobbing in and out of the rush of faces. The stout figure in the white *kurta* and pajamas blended in and out of the open shops, first disappearing among heaps of colored cloth, then emerging again onto the sidewalk, the small girl with the ponytail stepping quietly behind.

Okiri tried to keep his attention fixed on the Asian, but the market swirl of the shops around him kept drawing him away. This was not the drabness of a Nairobi crowd with blacks and whites both lost in the same European clothes. Instead, there was an extravagant wash of color that—to Okiri, raised in high country—seemed at one with the thick, tangible air and with the sun that here seemed closer to earth than in the highlands. Everything mingled and lost distinctness. Africans blended into Asians, Arabs into Europeans, features and skin color losing stability. In this strange African city with an Arab quarter and a Portuguese fort, with a jumbled past seething with Parsis and Englishmen, Muslims and infidels, Africans and Arabs, race and religion no longer seemed a badge, but a secret to be learned. Muslim tailors with bead caps and mottled skin arched over sewing machines, their bare feet racing the treadles. Men with Asian faces and African hair sat on high stools behind open counters of ivory and spice, perfumes and silk. Amid piles of red carpets and stacks of brass-bound chests brought by the dhows, they bargained with tall black men in Muslim robes who spoke a Swahili pure and elegant beyond the hopes of a detective from the Lake Province.

It was this ease of language that amazed Okiri more than anything else. He had learned Swahili as a third language, after his own tribal tongue and English. Swahili was a language of his profession: a dialect in which to give orders and interrogate prisoners, something as coarse and useful as a roughly made tool. But the coastal people spoke Swahili with song and clarity. Their speech was full of strange words and proverbs that Okiri only dimly understood, but the rhythm and rhyme of which filled him with admiration. When he spoke with them in their native language he felt tongue-tied and ashamed, the way he had felt in the presence of his grandparents, when he realized that his years in English-speaking schools had robbed him of the old words of his own tribal tongue. Compared to the elders of his family—as to these Swahili merchants—Okiri felt his own speech was flat and pale.

As he leaned against a doorway, watching the Asian buy the little girl a spray of yellow flowers, the detective felt a sudden jab at his kidneys. Instinctively he whirled and swung his hand. He heard a snap of wood, then a clattering on the floor of the shop in which he stood.

"What is this? No one is fighting, big man. Look at this. You will pay, right now." Naked to the waist, a thin African, his ribs echoing down his torso, was leaning over a broken ebony cane on the floor. "How do you expect people to see my goods if you lounge in the doorway? If you want to sleep, go to the park. Not here."

Okiri bent over to help the man pick up the pieces of the broken cane.

"Don't touch anything," the shopkeeper shouted, pushing Okiri's hands away from the bits of wood. "You've done enough, already."

"I'm sorry, *bwana*. I was working," said the inspector, chagrined. He fumbled for his wallet and showed the man his badge. The thin man grumbled and studied Okiri's face. Then he tapped two fingers against his palm. "Twenty-five shillings. Cash, no chits."

Okiri extracted the bills and passed them to the shopkeeper.

"You could have hurt me with your hands, *askari*," the store-keeper said, staring at the money. "I did nothing wrong."

Okiri paced back and forth before the doorway like an impatient house cat. Trying to placate the shopkeeper, he had lost sight of Bimji. He waved his hand distractedly at the thin man, a gesture halfway between a farewell and the shooing of a fly, and ran out to the sidewalk. Skirting a pushcart, he leaped over a high curb and walked down the street.

At the first corner he peered into a residential alleyway that led off from the street of shops. It was empty except for a sleeping dog. Quickly Okiri ran to the next block, his gaze still high and distant, scanning the crowd of shoppers. Twisting his way through the passersby, Okiri felt awkward and ungainly, like a young boy learning to hunt, imperfectly imitating the tracking glide of his elders. His feet were too big; his arms, too heavy. At the second corner he turned a few yards down the side street, as much to escape the irritated stare of the onlookers as in hope of finding the Asian and the girl.

Standing in the middle of the pitted pavement catching his breath, he saw a flash of white silk in a doorway a hundred yards down the block, and then, more clearly, Bimji's bulky figure knocking at a door. The girl, who had been so quiet in movement before, was excited now. She skipped and laughed, pulling at her uncle's sleeve. Okiri approached the pair, trying to rein his interest into the leisurely stroll of a passerby. As he neared, he saw the carved wooden door slowly open. An African boy about seventeen appeared in the doorway in a white undershirt, with a bright yellow and brown *kikoi* wrapped around his waist. He bowed his head slightly as Bimji spoke indistinct words, then retreated back into the hallway.

Okiri leaned into a narrow passageway between two high, windowless, stucco walls. The slide down into Bimji's garbage pit in Kigeli still chastened the inspector, and his glances at the street were timid and hesitant. He saw only fragments of the scene that followed. First, a middle-aged Asian couple stood in the doorway: the man was smaller and thinner than Bimji, the woman nearly as big as the hotel keeper. At the inspector's next glance the small girl was embracing the large woman. Her thin arms were clasped tight around the ample waist, pulling the loosely fitting sari through which Okiri could glimpse folds of brown flesh. Bimji's hand, still resting on his niece's shoulder, lifted to take from the sidewalk a plastic shopping bag bulging with parcels and pass it to the African boy, who led the family back into the hidden courtyard of the home.

As they disappeared from Okiri's sight, the parents and child were absorbed in their greetings, lost in one another. Bimji walked apart, steps behind, clasping and unclasping his thick hands behind his back, nervous darkness playing on his features. Just before he stepped inside the doorway his eyes met Okiri's and held for an instant. There was fright and resignation in the Asian's gaze. He looks like a prisoner in the dock, thought the inspector, then dismissed the idea as his own invention. It is only my height that he notices. I am merely a stranger. In the same moment the two men dropped their glance. The Asian threw back his shoulders and walked inside the door.

Okiri stepped out into the street, and, after a moment's hesitation, walked to a cluster of pushcarts that had gathered back where the alleyway met the main street. He bought a cup of tea, the steaming brew poured from the long spout of a vendor's brass pot.

For three more hours Okiri walked the short Old Town street, keeping his eye on Bimji's brother's doorway. He saw the African servant emerge with an empty sack of cheap rainbow plastic under his arm, then return loaded with fresh produce: swollen ripe mangoes, tomatoes, purple onions, and small yellow pumpkins. Half an hour later the boy was out a second time and came back with two hens, their feet bound with twine, their tail feathers limp in the mid-afternoon humidity. The servant appeared discontented with his task. He frowned to himself, muttering words under his breath, wiping his brow with his hand, then shaking the drops of moisture to the pavement. The fabric of the *kikoi* began to cling to his legs as tightly as a bar girl's skirt.

Okiri stopped drinking tea the third time the houseboy came out. He had drunk nine or ten cups without thinking. The vendor eyed him with peaceful curiosity, backing off slightly each time he refilled the policeman's cup, as if he suspected an explosion. The tea had left Okiri edgy and restless, and when the servant came out—this time without a shopping bag—Okiri abandoned his post and followed him. The teenager seemed calmer now, although the afternoon had not cooled since his earlier trips. Without the multicolor sack, he no longer had the badge of a houseboy. There was a saunter to his walk, which before had been merely harried. His steps were quick, his pace determined. He stopped only once: to buy a Fanta at a corner cigarette shop.

Okiri followed him through the winding streets—out to Ndia Kuu Road, which ran along the dhow harbor, and then down the sloping beach of the Pwakuu, a sandy flatland littered with boulders, charred tin cans, and pools of muck left by the receding tide. Spaced out along the harbor's edge were five or six beached dhows, resting out of the water in rough cradles of mangrove poles, dismasted for repairs. Workers in shorts and bead caps paced back and forth between the exposed boats and jerry cans filled with a slimy mixture of beef fat and lime. They scooped the warm paste by the handful, smearing the sealant over the bare timbers of the dhows. Others ladled a pungent fish oil out of rusted barrels and polished the boats' rails until they glowed the same warm red-brown that Okiri remembered from the stools his grandfather had carved, in their homeland five hundred miles from the sea.

The servant from Bimji's brother's house stopped by a squatting man who was beating a drum, setting a languid rhythm for the workers. The houseboy's steps had lost their determination. Okiri watched him scan the work gangs until the boy spotted the man he was looking for, at the far end of the flat. Gathering the cloth of his *kikoi* in his fist, the servant ran down the beach, skirting the mine field of poles and barrels, until he came to a chocolate-colored man with massive arms and shoulders and a square skull shaven completely clean. The houseboy paused and stood respectfully to one side, while the bald man gave orders to a crew of workers. Then he presented himself to the older man. With every few words the bald man would nod, his eyes still on the workers in front of him, repairing the boat.

The exchange finished, the houseboy started to thread his way back to the avenue that rimmed the harbor. He was clambering up a bank of rocks, intent on his footing, when he felt Okiri's hand on his shoulder. Though surprised, he did not jump at the touch. Instead he froze, like a rabbit run down. Okiri uttered the word "policeman," and the boy wilted to the rocks, sitting on a boulder, his hands loose at his side.

"This is not about you. It is just information I want," said the inspector, but the words did not seem to calm the boy. Okiri stretched himself uneasily on a chain of rocks in the lee of the road embankment. He was trying to maintain a difficult balance between keeping his new trousers clean and not rolling down the slope to the tidal flat. Still, he felt that if he kept himself down at the houseboy's physical level, the teenager might talk more freely.

The inspector reached in his wallet and drew out a yellowed clipping from the *Daily Nation,* a fragment of a photograph of Bimji and local Kigeli officials at the opening of a gas station. The Asian's face was circled in red pencil, his features blurred by the pointillist newspaper reproduction. Although the photograph had been taken only a few months before, Okiri thought it looked ancient, like the vague pictures from the turn of the century in his secondary school history textbook of railway workers clustered around the body of a dead lion.

The boy told Okiri the part he already knew. Yes, that was his master's brother, who had come from upcountry with the little girl. "He eats too much. I keep having to go out to get things to fill him up. He is like a bucket that leaks."

"I hope he will not be staying with you long."

Okiri scrambled in his pocket for a piece of sweet gum to offer the boy. The servant studied it for a second, then eagerly stuck it in his mouth.

"That is the good thing. He leaves in the morning. That is why I had to talk with the *nakhoda*"—the boy gestured down to the beach—"the captain of my master's dhow." The servant poked between his teeth. "What is this thing?"

"Gum and sugar. It is like a sweet."

"It is not a narcotic?" The boy spoke the last word in English.

"No, it is like a sweet." Okiri put a stick in his own mouth to reassure him. "Bimji will be leaving on the dhow?"

"No. My master will go on the dhow with the *nakhoda*. After one more feast, of course"—the houseboy shifted on the rock, his sigh nearly swallowing the gum. "His brother goes by taxi to Malindi. Then the boat will meet him again, I think, somewhere on the beach. That is what I was to tell the captain, to get ready. They will meet him on the beach with the white man, the *mzungu.*"

Okiri started and tore a piece of his trousers on a sharp point of rock. "What white man?"

Caution entered the houseboy's words. "I don't know. I don't think my master knew of him either. He is a messenger of some kind. But he is a rich man—he has money."

"He is a rich messenger?"

The boy shrugged. He rolled his fingers in the edge of the *kikoi* he wore around his waist. "I don't understand all of this. They talk in their own language, the Indians' language."

"Gujerati," said Okiri in a little twitch of erudition.

"If you say so."

The boy shifted his bottom on the rocks. Below them, on the flat, the tide was creeping in, filling small, disconnected basins with dark water, then linking the low places together in a necklace of pools. Okiri watched the enlaced pattern that would last but a few minutes, then wash away under the small steady waves of the harbor.

"They think I don't understand it, but I am learning some words." The houseboy lifted his head back up and gazed out to the water with Okiri.

"Words like 'white man' and 'money'?"

The boy nodded, then lowered his head again, returning to the nervous adjustment of the cloth around his waist. He paused and looked the policeman directly in the eyes. Anxiety creased his forehead. "Do these things help you?" he asked. He was half open for approval, half closed in apprehension.

"A little."

Okiri stood up and shook loose the cloth of his pants, now coated with the muck of the harbor. Scanning the rocks, he picked up an old board with a single large nail driven through the center. He remembered the storekeeper and the cane. Okiri tapped the board against a boulder gently, the loose nail tinkling faintly like a tiny cymbal each time it struck.

"You know of course you must not speak of my questions to your master. You will tell him nothing."

The boy's eyes were fixed on the board and the tall, muscular man standing above him. Again he nodded at the detective's words.

163

"If not, I will break you myself." Suddenly Okiri swung the board up and smashed it against the boulder. The wood split, exploded, and clattered off down the slope to the water. "Remember, boy, I am the government."

The inspector could see the adolescent's fear. Swearing allegiance, the boy jumped up and ran across the rocks back to the street.

Okiri was left alone on his boulder, with the broken board in his hand. He stared at the shredded wood a second, then tossed it over his shoulder. He knew it had been a cheap trick, but the inspector was still rather proud of himself. Feeling smug and a little sheepish, he crossed over the shrinking beach and headed back toward Fort Jesus. To preserve what little dignity the pants had left, he lifted the cuffs of his trousers above the encroaching tide.

OKIRI SPENT THAT evening across from the house of Bimji's brother. He didn't want to lose the Asian. A sudden squall had blown in from the ocean, and the first gusts of cool wind had sent shutters clapping up and down the street. Fat raindrops from the darkened sky streaked down the stucco of the high housefronts, swirling over the crenellated tops. Within five minutes the alleyway was a torrent. Okiri shielded his head as best he could with a crumpled newspaper and pressed himself against the side of the alley in the shelter of a house's narrow eaves. Next to him a red concrete gutterspout gurgled into the street.

Strange things floated down the alleyway: palm fronds, a ring of keys, a live rat pawing frantically to keep its head above the tide. Okiri perched his feet on a narrow ledge that lined the bottom of the blank wall next to him and kept his toes above water. His earlier concern at the beach for the press of his trousers was pointless now. Coated in the warm rain, he peered at the windows of the house across the street.

The houseboy, who had appeared in the doorway at the first drops of rain, had left one window open. The shutter was still flapping sharply in the wind. Okiri knew it was a gesture directed at him, though in fact it helped him little. He could see nothing inside: only occasional flares of lantern light and a darkened hallway. Between flushes of rain, sudden bursts of loud laughter against the clink of dishes came from down the corridor. To Okiri, the laughter sounded too loud. It was a kind of nervous, overbearing laughter that verged on pain.

164

Okiri cautioned himself that these things were difficult for him to judge. The laughter of Asians and Europeans, like their tears, was often different from that of Africans. His own people restrained their laughter more, and their grief less, than these others. To find the real meaning of these wordless sounds required interpretations that his dictionaries did not provide. More than with his training, Okiri had to listen with his instincts.

When the rain stopped, stars appeared above the alley. The houseboy came back to the windows, throwing open the shutters. He did not look at Okiri. From inside the house, the sounds of the meal ceased. The inspector heard only the barks of dogs and, dying away, the racing of the rainwater through the gutters. The lanterns faded on the street.

For a moment, Okiri was torn between waiting the night out in the alleyway and retiring back downtown to find a bed. Then he discarded the latter idea. The evening had been freshened by the brief, heavy rain. The sky was warm and quiet. There would be something too dreary in seeking out a cheap hotel, and Okiri was intent on keeping Bimji within his sight. As the lights went out in the house across the street, the inspector walked back to the fort where he had left the Capri, enjoying the stretch of muscle in his legs.

With only the yellow fog lights lit, he circled the car back to the alley on Bimji's brother's street. Then, parked in the shadows, he opened the windows to admit the night breeze and curled his long body against the seat to rest. He was not tired. For hours his eyes did not close, except for brief moments of dreamless sleep that rested him like breaths. He lay there peacefully the whole night, waiting for the sounds of morning life from the Asian's home and the first flash of dawn from over the sea.

CHAPTER XVIII

IT HURT ELLEN to watch Grimes's face. He kept trying to apologize to her with his eyes. She could barely see anything more of his face than his eyes, through the matted hair and stubble. Answering Mathenge's questions, he had taken on the extreme appearance of some of those lost Englishmen—drunks mostly—who worked at menial jobs in the smaller African towns. Without family or connections, haggard and unshaven, they were not people who, as the missionaries sniffed, had "gone native," but rather total isolates who had retreated long ago into a country of their own imagining. In his fear, Grimes had no consciousness of the way he looked.

His appearance, surprisingly, helped with Mathenge. The minister in his pin-striped suit could not believe that a man with so little self-regard could be up to deceiving someone of Mathenge's own importance. And the elastic bandage had disarmed him. While the wrist itself, sprained in the fight with Moguru, had healed, the bandage was caked with the dust of the dozen roads he had taken from Kigeli to the sea. Grimes had forgotten about it. If it were indeed the badge of a murderer, presumed the minister, rather than the aftereffect of a drunken brawl, the American would hardly display such insouciance.

Grimes's answers to Mathenge's questions were short and correct, less out of self-discipline than from an abiding fatigue. Though they had spent only a few seconds together alone, Grimes's and Ellen's stories matched. Grimes had made the same calculation as she. They had both told the truth.

Mathenge summoned a towel, basin, and mirror for his new prisoner, then left the room. Grimes studied himself in the glass.

Fruitlessly he ran his fingers through his hair and across the two days' growth on his cheeks, then gave up.

"You didn't know you looked like that?" She frowned.

"No. I washed my face at Berryman's, but I guess I wasn't seeing anything. No wonder he acted the way he did. He must have thought he'd let the wild man of Borneo into his house."

Grimes searched the room, then walked over to collapse against the wall, on the narrow cot. "It's like I've been staring down a tunnel ever since I left you at Kongoru."

Ellen crossed the concrete floor and sat down beside him. She placed her hand gently against his cheek. "You notice they've given us just the one bed."

"I think he wants to loosen us up." Grimes rubbed his eyebrow. A fine dust came off onto his fingers. Ellen smiled.

"Or maybe kill one of us before it's time to go to sleep."

Leaving him to soak in the possibility, Ellen got up and walked to the table. "Do you want a drink? Kimathi brought two glasses."

Grimes shook his head. He could barely keep his eyes open. A pleasing lethargy was folding over him, which the strange name held back only for an instant. "Kimathi?" he asked.

"The little man who brought you here." Ellen sat down on the bed with her own tumbler as Grimes nodded slowly. "He seems to specialize in deliveries."

Ellen told Grimes about her kidnapping and interrogation, nuns and all. As she spoke, he retrieved the battered Santa Claus mask from his jeans and rested the loose rubber face over his knee.

"I wonder what kind of books he reads."

"Who knows? One of my students collects baseball cards. She's never seen the game. She picked it up from a Catholic Charities pen pal somewhere." Ellen shrugged her shoulders as if she were chilled. "It's all culture shock, Jonathan, his and ours."

Grimes turned Ellen's face toward him. He kissed her on the forehead. "I should never have told you about any of this. I should never have gotten you involved. I'm sorry."

Gently she returned his kiss. Her cheek brushed the harsh stubble of his own as their lips drew apart. "It's not what you told me, Jonathan. It's what you did and what Bimji did. They didn't care what I knew when they brought me here. It was to get a hold on you. It's probably saved my life so far that I had any story at all to tell Mathenge. If I had known nothing, he wouldn't have believed me. Now he thinks he's accomplished something."

Once more they embraced. Grimes's hand ran to Ellen's breast, caressing through the damp, thin cloth of her blouse. Then, as their eyes went to the door and they again heard the unhurried footsteps from the hall, they retreated, embarrassed, awkward. Making love here would be a performance. They adjusted the thin sheeting, and, fully clothed, their bodies frustrated, clinging to each other, they fell asleep.

HALF AN HOUR later, as the new dawn lit the sky above the courtyard outside the window, Kimathi's key turned in the lock. Purple bruises still swelled the little man's face. "You," he said, pointing at Grimes with a jangling ring of keys. "Just you, not the woman. I am waiting."

Grimes put on his shoes and shuffled to his feet. Somehow, without touching him, Kimathi made Grimes look as though he were being dragged somewhere in the jaws of a predator. Then the door slammed behind them.

A minute later, Ellen heard footsteps in the courtyard beyond the window. Mathenge was sitting at the edge of the well. Grimes stood before him with Kimathi at his side, the small man nonchalantly holding a pistol in his hand. For an hour, the minister and the American exchanged words, Mathenge speaking in harsh, low whispers that Ellen could not make out. Again and again the minister spoke, and Grimes—his back to Ellen and the barred window—nodded. Suddenly Mathenge walked off toward the water and Kimathi, prodding Grimes's ribs with the pistol, led him out of Ellen's sight.

When he returned to their cell, Ellen anxiously searched his eyes. "No bruises."

"I know. I was watching you."

For a moment Grimes was embarrassed. He felt exposed, compromised. He splashed some water from the basin on his face, wiped it clean, then poured himself a tumbler of gin. Sunlight coursed through the single window. Above the water, the shore birds made their morning noise. Grimes slumped to the bed.

Apprehensively, still standing, Ellen hovered over her lover. "What are you going to have to do for him?"

"Go ahead as planned. I'm to meet Bimji at the same place with the money." He bit his lip, then smiled wanly. "They didn't let you know where we are when you came, did they?"

"No, I was blindfolded."

"It turns out we're north of Malindi, about three or four miles from where Bimji and I are supposed to rendezvous with his brother's boat. I don't think Bimji knew that. He wouldn't have enjoyed the proximity." Grimes swirled the bitter gin in his glass and swallowed it whole.

"Did Bimji know about Mathenge?"

"I'm not sure. I don't know how much he knew about Moguru. I don't know why he killed Moguru or even if he did. Anyway, he'll find out about Mathenge soon enough now. I'm going to introduce them to each other."

"Bimji must have known Moguru had something to do with Section 21."

"Maybe. He may have been both a little more naive and a little more decent than I'd thought."

"How can you say that after what he's put you through, Jonathan? Christ! After what he's put both of us through?"

"You don't understand. They've got Moguru's body." As Ellen retreated to the window, Grimes shifted in his seat on the bed. "Someone called the police, and they found it in back of Bimji's hotel."

Ellen looked at Grimes's agitated face. Distrust sparked in her eyes.

"Don't you understand? My knife wasn't in the body. It was nowhere near my house." Grimes leaned over in the bed and grabbed the iron railing. "Bimji was doing me a favor. He trusted me. He must have carried the body out there when he left Kigeli. He didn't put the frame on me even before he knew I'd get the money to him."

Ellen stared out the narrow window. Her voice was distracted, distant. "So he doesn't have a hold on you anymore."

"For what it's worth. It's not Bimji I'm worried about now. It's the man out there." Grimes put the glass to his mouth, then angrily threw the empty tumbler into the corner. There was no smash. The thick glass held together before softly cracking, as if Grimes's rage was insufficient to disturb it.

Ellen began to pace back and forth in the small room, straining inside it. She was making no effort to contain the anger growing inside her. "When will all this happen?"

"Just when Bimji scheduled. I was to meet him sometime tonight around 2 A.M., when both the beach and the sea would be empty. I'll be there. And so will Mathenge and Kimathi."

170

"Isn't he worried that you'll spoil it for him?"

"No. He trusts me now. That's another gift from Bimji. Finding Moguru's body more or less where I said it was seems to prove I was telling him the truth. Which I was. I had no reason to protect Bimji then." Grimes searched in vain for another glass. He motioned to take a swig from the bottle itself, then stopped in mid-gesture, rebuking himself, and put the liquor back on the table.

"Do you think you have reason to protect him now?"

"He didn't carry through on the threat. I'm not that sure I want to sell him out to Mathenge."

"You don't have a choice, Jonathan, if you want us to stay alive." Ellen cut her words, hard as glass. Her face grew dark.

Grimes got up and took the bottle, a long drink this time that burned the bottom of his throat. He sat back down, defeated. "I know you're right. It's just that I'm not certain we'll stay alive even if I do go through with it. What sense would it make to him to let us go?"

"Some. Quiet Americans would cause him less trouble than disappearing Americans."

"You're certain?"

"Of course not."

Grimes shook his head equivocally. A long silence passed. Then he reached under his shirt and unstrapped the Asian's wallet. "Mathenge let me keep this for a while—since I'm not going anywhere without him." Idly he counted out the piles of notes wrapped in plastic bags and placed them on the table: dollars, pounds, Kenyan shillings. He stared at the worn, ancient bills, the currency not of Nairobi banks, but of small-town hustles and midnight negotiations: the back room exchange. Here, with Mathenge's men outside the door, it was useless.

"Do you want to play cards?" he asked Ellen, a gesture of truce. He picked up the fresh deck that had come with the morning gin bottle. Ellen said nothing but stayed at the window, staring out to sea, her back toward her lover. Grimes unwrapped one of the piles of Bimji's notes and, cutting the deck, dealt the money and cards slowly to himself.

AN OLDER MAN, mumbling constantly to himself, served them a tray of dinner. Kimathi seemed to have gone from the hallway, though twice they heard his voice, indistinct, through the courtyard window, and then fading steps. The meal was a pile of whole fried fish with tiny grimaces on their faces. They were given no silverware—"Security," Ellen said—and, as they ate with their fingers, the blend of the old grease and the fresh fish left a disturbing and contradictory taste in their mouths.

After the old man took their plates away, the sun fell behind the inland hills, and the air and sea grew still. In the driveway, a car started and pulled away. No voices came from the other rooms of Mathenge's home. The sporadic tingling and water sounds of the kitchen across the courtyard disappeared. They seemed alone, sealed in the house, abandoned by their captors. Grimes awaited Mathenge's summons, circling the small table, glancing at his watch, while Ellen sat still on the bed, leafing through the ancient magazines left for them. She looked at them without reading, or even seeing, like someone reciting a rote prayer, drained of meaning. Out the window, they could see nothing but the faint gray of beach and the dark silhouettes of the palms, beginning to catch motion in the nightly shift of wind from land to sea. The trunks creaked in the breeze, a soft groaning.

A key turning in the door lock broke the spell. The sound of the tumblers falling seemed to come from a place completely alien. It had nothing to do with what had gone before—Ellen's enforced lethargy, Grimes's faulty patience. The prisoners stiffened at the sound, but it was not Mathenge or Kimathi in the doorway. A woman Grimes had never seen before stood at the entrance to the room, her hands tight around a ring of keys. Her eyes paid no attention to him. Instead, she walked to Ellen and grabbed her wrist, pulling her up from the bed.

"You. Come with me."

"I don't understand."

"It's simple. I'm letting you go. Get your things." The African woman scanned the small cell, distaste on her features, as if she were sniffing a piece of meat no longer fit to eat.

"Things? I don't have any things." The surprise in Ellen's voice only partially masked her anger. "Your husband's friends hardly let me pack."

"I am not responsible for them." There was no emotion on Mukami's face.

As the two women spoke, Grimes stood in the corner, following their words. Ellen motioned to him to take up his backpack. Mukami shook her head vigorously.

"Only you. He cannot go."

Ellen froze where she was standing. "Why not?" But for the

172

tension in her muscles and the memory of Mathenge himself, she felt as if she were in a government office, bracing to hear a petty bureaucrat explain why something could not be done.

"I can only risk so much, Miss Ferris. You have nothing to do with this business. It is between my husband and him." She pointed to Grimes. "If I let you go, Mathenge will be angry. He may send someone after you. He may not. But he will consider it within the range of my peculiarities. Your friend is different. I cannot take the chance."

"And what if we both walk out now? You have no weapon."

Mukami dropped the hand that was still clinging to Ellen's wrist. She took a step backward, but not out of fear. "Mathenge doesn't leave me alone here." She nodded her head slightly to the hallway behind her. The white-haired serving man stood rigidly against the wall, both hands clasped around an automatic. There was an intense, terrified concentration in his eyes, as if he were straining to see something a long distance away.

"He is not experienced in these things. I don't know whether that makes him more or less dangerous." Mukami could not restrain a smile. "If you were to sit down, it would calm him."

Grimes backed down the bed, letting his pack slip beside him. He fought to take his eyes away from the old man's pistol and look at Mukami. The African woman was relaxing now. Grimes watched the green and brown flash of her skirt, the strain of the cloth as she shifted her hips against the small table.

"If I go"—Ellen brushed a strand of hair from her forehead, hesitating—"and Jonathan stays, what will your husband do to him?"

Mukami tilted her head smoothly on her long neck and shrugged her shoulders. "It will depend on how well your friend performs his task and how frightened of my husband he seems to be. My husband likes people who are frightened of him. He likes us all to be predictable." Mukami rubbed the smooth skin of her shoulders. "Of course, that is advice, not a prediction."

"Would he be less likely to hurt Jonathan if I stayed with him?"

Mukami laughed. "No, not at all. He might feel more sorry afterward. I think it would just cause him more trouble. He would say, now there are two of you to keep quiet and that would make him more frightened of you. He would like you even less."

"Ellen," Grimes's voice was low, cracking, insistent. "Go. Maybe you can get—" He stopped abruptly.

"Don't guard your tongue on my account. Please feel free to

173

speak." Mukami was still laughing, but her tone was now soft, flirting. "I don't care what you do to get him out, Miss Ferris. Just don't involve me."

Uncertain, Grimes glanced at Ellen, then spoke in clumsy French. *"Tu peux faire un rendez-vous avec le bâteau du frère de Bimji. Il doit être près d'ici."*

Ellen nodded. She walked to his side and leaned over. Softly, they kissed.

"Let us go, Miss Ferris. My husband will come back soon."

Again Mukami took Ellen by the wrist and led her into the hallway as the white-haired man sealed the door behind them.

It was Ellen's first glimpse of the interior of the house. The walls of the hallway, and of the row of small rooms into which she could see, were of a smooth white plaster. They were covered with Nubian platters woven from coils of thick straw and suspended from dark nails. The parade of brightly colored spirals dizzied Ellen as she looked at them, the colors blending and fighting in her sight. As she turned her eyes from them she could see Mukami beside her, her grip tightening on Ellen's wrist. Mathenge's wife was somehow more apprehensive outside the prison room than she had been inside. She beckoned the old man to precede them, as if the white-haired servant with his pistol could protect them against the return of Kimathi or his own master.

At the end of the corridor Mukami opened a Dutch door studded with brass nails. At the creak of hinges, starlight and sea wind poured into the narrow hallway from outside the frame of dark wood. Ellen looked out at the courtyard with the well, and beyond, to the line of palms and the sea. The windows around the courtyard—except for the single square of grillwork that kept Grimes from her—were dark. Pale points of moonlight danced from the roll of breakers at the edge of the beach. Suddenly Mukami hissed, "Go quickly!" and the door was closed, then locked, behind Ellen.

"Go quickly!" Again Mukami's words insisted from behind the wood, and Ellen dashed across the courtyard to the grove of palms. When she reached the clear sand, still running, she turned left, north up the beach. Her sandals slid under her feet. She stumbled, unseeing, straining to get out beyond the sight of Mathenge's house. For five minutes she ran, expecting flashlights behind her or shots or even—in the seconds when she gave in to the panic that lay just beneath her thoughts—the baying of dogs. Then she stopped, out of breath, a dull fire in her calves. Sitting in the sand, she cradled her head between her knees, and the night, which had shattered into dizzying points of light, reassembled.

Her faintness subsided. Looking south along the beach, back from where she had fled, Ellen could no longer separate the grove of trees that hid Mathenge's house from the line of palms that smoothly paralleled the shoreline. The land and distance had swallowed it up. To the north, up the beach, the sand stretched out white in the moonlight until it curved and ended at an immense boulder that rose out of the beach like a giant ship. Water from the breakers eased against the rock's seaward edge, splashing a thin line of white foam in the night. She recalled Grimes's words from the afternoon. It was at the rock that Bimji would be waiting for the American.

Ellen felt for the watch on her wrist and started as the crystal gave to her touch. She looked at the watch face, cracked, a layer of sand smeared against the numerals. She must have broken it in the run, swinging her arm against a tree trunk or a rock in the dash for the open beach. She had no memory of it. But then she had no memory of any part of the run. It was as if she had sprung instantly from Mathenge's doorway to this bare stretch of sand.

The watch read half past midnight; it could not have been stopped for more than a few minutes. She would have perhaps an hour to get up the beach and, if it were close enough to the shore, reach Bimji's brother's boat. She stood up and, brushing the sand from her skirt, walked to the edge of the water. Sandals in her hand, she let the smooth water rush over her feet. The ocean was warm, the breakers gentle and steady. Behind the palms inland, she could see no lights, though at some point, she knew, there must be a road. It might be a few hundred yards, or a few miles, from the shore. Even if she could find it, where could she go? There was no point in getting the police. Mathenge was the police.

Ellen walked a few feet deeper into the sea, tucking the sandals into her waistband and letting the hem of her thin cotton skirt trail in the water. A cluster of lights twinkled on the ocean's near horizon. It would not be impossible to swim to a vessel offshore. If one of those lights should draw nearer the shore up by the rock, it would have to be the boat of Bimji's brother. She had crossed Vermont lakes longer than the distance it would take.

Retreating a few paces, she began to walk in the half-light along the border of sea and beach, up to the solitary boulder. Ellen kept to the ribbon of wet, firm sand, where her steps were easy. She had no idea if she could reach the rock in time, nor if the boat would be there. She knew there would be no assurance that Bimji's brother would help them, even if she reached him before the rendezvous. He might try to intercept Bimji and leave Jonathan to Mathenge's frustration. Or he might merely flee himself, abandoning his brother. Finally, there was the possibility of his not believing Ellen at all, although, Ellen thought ruefully, he could not ignore her. Fishing a half-dressed white woman from the sea would certainly gain his attention.

Still, there was no other chance. Again, Ellen looked to the east and scanned the sea. At the cluster of beacons, a single red light seemed to grow big and pull off the horizon toward the shore ahead of her. Though in her heart she suspected the light was more hope than vision, Ellen pulled the sandals from her waistband. Dropping them in the sand, she walked to the water. With long, smooth strokes, she began to swim across the gentle sea.

CHAPTER XIX

BIMJI RENTED A bicycle in Malindi. He went straight from the taxi stand to a beachfront shed where the bicycle man offered him a choice between a Raleigh and an Anchor. The Anchors looked just like the English Raleighs but were made by the Chinese and rented for ten shillings a day less. Bimji indulged himself. He took one of the Raleighs, a three-speed.

He rode it back and forth on the gravel a few yards and started sinking with the seatpost as he pedaled. The rental man was waiting with a wrench when Bimji pushed the bike back to the shed. He lifted the seat back up, tightened the nuts, and, like a cautious father, gave the Asian a little starting shove. The man studied the Asian's wavering progress down the avenue until, confident Bimji would stay aloft on his own, he busied himself with his other repairs.

Okiri, watching from across the way, pulled the Capri into a gas station and asked for a full tank. There was little danger of losing Bimji, tottering slowly along the flat avenue ahead of him. The detective, leaning against the car's hood, could still see nearly a mile down the long beachfront road, quiet in the late afternoon. The Asian was bobbing along the line of asphalt in a pattern that, although it seemed as random as a fly's walk on a plaster wall, made its way steadily north.

Okiri stretched his legs beside the gas pump. Following Bimji's taxi up the coast road had not been restful. The car's destination had been certain, but the path it followed—given the limited options in country where there was essentially one road—was amazingly erratic. The driver had left the road all along the way to deliver packages at obscure houses. The parcels were irregular patchworks of brown paper that, Okiri became convinced, must be bunches of soccer balls tied with rags and string. Each delivery was accompanied by the time it took the driver to share a pot of tea with the grateful recipients. Outside, Bimji and the other passengers, not privy to the gratitude, waited in the taxi, swatting flies and shifting their bottoms on the damp seats. Okiri, diffidently down the road, tried to stay awake.

Once on the main road, the driver would push the vehicle forward in bursts of recklessness that Okiri could barely keep pace with, only to slow suddenly down to a crawl. What Okiri had hoped would be a pleasant ride along the seacoast had taken on the unpleasant taste of a police training exercise. The nervous excitement he had felt in Mombasa, when he sensed he was drawing near the center of the maze he had entered in Kigeli, now dissipated into a pair of road-weary knees.

Okiri watched the clicking of the gauge, still keeping his eye out for Bimji. The boy was handpumping the gas with a long pole, pausing after each motion to rest. Just when the inspector was afraid the Asian might disappear from sight he saw Bimji stop at the front of a stucco hotel, get off the bike and then on again, reversing direction. Slowly the bicyclist began to make his way back to the gas station, now sometimes lost in the soft shadow of the setting sun. Okiri paid his money and slid into the driver's seat of the dusty Ford. The Asian must be riding for the pleasure of it, he thought. He wants to see the ocean waves roll in on the beach. He is waiting.

I shall wait, too. Okiri spun the car out into the road and drove a few hundred yards down the highway in the direction of Bimji's bicycle, braking to watch a cluster of German tourists walk along the beach in white hats and khaki shorts. They clung to each other, almost in formation, with airline bags stuffed with towels over their shoulders, winding their way through the folded nets and beached prows of the fishing boats scattered along the sand. Okiri pulled the car over, opened the door to extend his legs, and leaned back in the seat. He tried to read the faces of the tourists, but he could not see their eyes, only cheeks puffed with sunburn underneath patches of shadow. Instead, Okiri watched their bodies. The striped shirts of the men could not hide their fat bellies; the women walked in a defiant near-nudity that had little of the erotic about it. The skin of their thighs was as soft as that of their faces was hard. The tourists made Okiri think of fire ants parading across a meadow, circling stumps, avoiding obstacles. It was the way they skirted the fishermen and their boats, methodically leaving space between themselves and the Africans.

The white man who was Bimji's "rich messenger" would not be like these, Okiri thought, but someone whose stay in Africa was longer. He searched his memory for the names of the two men the talk in Kigeli had linked with the Asian: Landers and Grimes, the hunter and the teacher. But Landers was dead. He had seen the hunter's corpse himself. And Grimes? Grimes was on vacation, they had said at his school. He was called away.

The houseboy in Mombasa had told the dhow captain to prepare for a voyage of several days. If Bimji were trying to leave the country—up the coast to Somalia or Djibouti, or down to Lourenço Marques or Durban—perhaps he was afraid to carry his own money. The schoolteacher might be the one to help him. If Bimji had killed Landers—who the rumors said had poached the skins and tusks Bimji was selling—he would want to flee. But then what did Kimathi and the Section have to do with him? And what about Moguru, the other teacher who had come here to buy land and whom no one had seen, the husband of the peculiar woman who had given him the carved stool?

Okiri ferreted among the loose folders, old newspapers, and oil cans that littered the back seat of the Capri. The stool was nestled in a tire tube that curled about it like a fat, protective snake. As he looked at it now, the bit of wood was cruder, less beautiful, than he had remembered it. The ends of the three small legs were chipped; the seat was marred as if someone had drawn a thick knife blade across it. There was nothing about it to attract the German tourists: neither the brazen picturesqueness of airport art—the thick-lipped women's heads that seemed to shout *"Africa,"* even when the word itself was not in fact painted across the base—nor any of the elegance of the work of the real carvers.

But Okiri found it soothing just to hold it in his hands. It made him think of the herdsmen of his own people, sitting on the plains, in still communion with their cattle. They carried in such a piece of burnished wood a resting place more secure than any that men like Bimji or Kimathi could know—the one, an anxious exile; the other, Mathenge's tool, deformed forever by his servitude.

The Asian's restlessness would bring them all together. Okiri was certain of it, with the certainty of something one has dreamed. Mathenge and Kimathi, the schoolteacher, himself. Bimji was too frightened to protect himself. His fear encumbered him, slowing him with his own haste. He was taking Okiri with him and—in some way Okiri had not fully divined—Mathenge as well. They were racing together through underbrush, entangled.

Okiri wrapped the stool in a soft, clean rag and placed it back on the floor of the Capri's rear seat. On the beach, the Germans had disappeared into the thatched cabanas of their hotel. The fishermen, talking, laughing, some swinging kerosene lanterns in their hands, were returning to the town in twos and threes. Distant along the street, the entangled man still pedaled back and forth in the dying twilight. Okiri's eyes followed him as he traced and retraced his path, a furious motion in his feet. The detective walked to the back of the Capri, opened the trunk, and pulled out his own ancient bicycle.

THE MEAL TASTED sour in the Asian's mouth. It did nothing to ease the tiredness in his legs, the core of muscles a bundle of fatigue smaller than the bulk of his thighs. The resort menu was some Englishman's idea of food—the same kind of slop, Bimji realized with a twinge, he often had served to tourists at his own hotel: pale vegetables, thin gravy, gray meat. He was alone now. He permitted himself to be disgusted with the food. It was something he had never allowed himself before. He pushed the plate aside and asked the waiter for a cup of coffee to burn away the taste, then added sweet biscuits to the order, something he hoped would cleanse his mouth.

Bimji looked around him. He was the only non-European in the dining room, except for the African waiters. There was a babel of strange North European languages at the tables near him and faces with long, pinched noses like those of Masai warriors—except the skin of these faces, if not burned red by the sun, was light, the hair blond.

He rubbed his legs. The bicycle ride had delighted him. His balance had returned from the days as a child when he had ridden errands for his father. By the time he was ready to eat, he was not half bad at it. He was proud of his control of the machine. In general, he was not good with machines. That was why he had never learned to drive a car and had hired a driver to take him on his errands around Kigeli. On the more sensitive journeys, Landers had driven him in his Land Rover. The hunter had taken him out to meet Moguru that night, out by the dry river, to the place where Landers buried the tusks.

The waiter brought Bimji bitter coffee in a tiny cup and a saucer of biscuits. The two men exchanged neither glances nor words. The biscuits were stale and slightly damp in the sea breeze that came through the long, open, harbor window, but the motion of his jaws, the mere movements of eating, were enough to give him pleasure.

It was better tonight that he not have a car. It would be easier to slip out of the town north to the spot where Grimes would be waiting. He knew there had been someone following him all along, on the train, in Nairobi. Even in his brother's street in Mombasa, he had felt eyes on him. But he had expected this. It was better that those eyes be on him than on Grimes.

He was confident Grimes would be there on the beach if no one else stopped him. The business with Moguru's body had frightened him sufficiently. Bimji had seen that in Grimes's face, in his hands. Grimes would be prepared to take unaccustomed risks. He would not think quickly enough to check back in Kigeli to see if Bimji had carried out his threat.

The Asian sipped his coffee; it tightened the lining of his mouth. He had hauled the body from the freezer himself. He had taken it as far from the hotel as he could before his strength gave out, before his revulsion at the task became greater than his desire to protect himself. There was nothing really to protect. He would have disappeared by the time the killing was traced to him. He had no concern for his reputation in Kigeli. He had never been beloved. Now he would be a monster with which to frighten children. It would be a kind of fame. He no longer cared about such things.

Even the fact that he was being followed worried him little, now that Meera had been returned to her parents. Bimji had no fear of lone policemen. In groups they could be terrible: gangs that found delight in the beating of petty thieves. But he had only contempt for a single one. On their own, they were cautious, as fearful of overstepping bounds as junior clerks in a government office. And whoever was driving the battered Capri that had trailed him from Mombasa would have difficulty following him on a bicycle at night through the rocks and dunes that guarded the Mambrui beach. He would be fifteen minutes behind. When he came to the beach, Bimji would be gone.

But Grimes would still be there. Bimji felt a twinge of remorse. Grimes was a weak man, but there was no point in exploiting him. He had done what he was told. Of course, there really was no need to expose him to the danger. He could take the schoolteacher with him to the boat and drop him off further down the coast. It was a splendid solution.

Bimji paid for his meal, and left the hotel with new buoyancy. He was happy to see himself as the American's protector. It gave him that same sense of control he had felt when conquering the bicycle. His age, the weight and decay of his body, none of these made any difference. There was nothing he was unable to do if he applied his intelligence. Nothing. Nothing at all.

OKIRI RODE DOWN the gravel road without turning on the flashlight tied to his handlebars. The road was glowing by itself, a phosphorescent whiteness against the shoulders of darker sand. Ahead, the clothing of the fat man on his bicycle also glowed as if painted, smooth. The bicyclists had no momentum. The gravel stopped them whenever they paused, and the man in front, older, heavier, paused often. He seemed unaware of Okiri, but the detective gave him several hundred yards, and pulled to the brush on the inland side of the road each time the Asian stopped for breath. When the trees thickened, in a shallow depression in the sand, the merchant seemed to fall off his bicycle. Okiri saw him lean out to the side as if turning, but stay there, folding down slowly like the page of a book read outdoors, sinking in a faint wind. In the blink of an eye, he was gone.

Okiri strained to see in the darkness. Ahead was the grove of palms in the road's dip, but Bimji had vanished. The detective waited a moment, caught between his fear of losing the Asian and his desire not to follow too closely, then pedaled after the track left by Bimji's bicycle. The line in the sand was like a snake's trail, its edge smearing outward at each point where the tires had slipped. Okiri followed it to the clump of trees, then it took a sudden turn directly into the brush that bordered the beach. It stopped abruptly amid a cluster of brambles. Okiri left his bicycle and poked into the bushes with his foot. He pulled Bimji's machine out of the underbrush, its front wheel spinning free as the detective dragged it loose.

Okiri listened for the Asian's footsteps, but he could hear nothing through the rhythm of the surf coming over the low dunes. The gravel held by the bushes was peppered, light and dark. The checkered bath of moonlight obscured it like a film that Okiri wished he could wipe from his eyes. He tried to find the man's footsteps leading away from the abandoned bicycle. Every faint disturbance of pebbles was a possibility.

Alone in the night, Okiri had no intuition of danger. He did not look behind him before bending over the ground and scanning the surface for a trace of Bimji's path. The African had not felt this calm before, this peacefulness. Drowsiness fogged his concentration; it was as if he had just awakened from an insufficient sleep.

The part of Okiri that calculated risks was surprised at the feeling. He was alone and unprotected in an unfamiliar landscape. None of his colleagues knew where he was, and none would have been with him if they had known. In a way that Okiri could decipher no more clearly than he could Bimji's footprints, the line the Asian was making in the sand led somehow to Okiri's superiors. Before Mathenge, there would be no one to help him but himself.

Yet it was his solitude that brought with it the calm in which Okiri moved. No eyes were upon him: not those of his family and clan, nor of the men with whom he worked, nor—and this he only suspected—those of his enemies. All his life the consciousness of those eyes had fed a vigilance that carried him outside of himself. With their absence came a freedom that showed itself as this sleepy peace, this sense of no danger that was a danger in itself.

For a moment, Okiri scuffed at the pebbles beneath his feet. He was not ready to admit to himself that Bimji's leaving his bicycle was an evasion, that the merchant knew he was being followed. He might only have decided to turn in across the deeper sand toward the water, where the bike would be useless. But even if Bimji knew of the man behind him, Okiri did not want to risk an open confrontation that might drive the Asian from his rendezvous with the *mzungu*.

Okiri had to find a vantage point where he would not be revealed to Bimji. The bare tops of the dunes to the detective's right were too open. But to the left, if he kept to the trees along the beach, he could reach a line of rocks that led down to a large boulder that rose where the sand met the sea. The brush and trees were on high land above the shoreline. From where the rocks started to fall down to the beach, he would be able to see the length of the shore for a few hundred yards in either direction.

The inspector left the Asian's bicycle where he had found it and set off toward the rocks, just behind the most shoreward line of palms. He bowed his head and leaned forward as he walked, although the trees were high enough to hide even Okiri's long form. The gesture was for his own self-discipline, to remind himself to be on guard against whoever lay hiding in the woods. From within the gabardine of his suit jacket he pulled out the American police-man's bowie knife in its stitched leather sheath. Strapping it to his belt, his fingers fumbled in the dark. The knife provided the same feeling—encumbered yet protected—he had felt when the school-teacher's wife gave him the stool in Kigeli. He rested his hand on the knife's handle and walked gingerly among the fallen twigs from the sand brush. Crabs skittered in the basins of smooth sand that dotted the path like puddles in the moonlight. From the shore, down the slope at his side, came the hiss of surf, the thick smell of seaweed and salt. The air tightened the skin at the base of his nostrils as a cloud of dust on the savannah might.

Okiri remembered the scent. When he had been a small boy, the first time they had given him charge of the family cattle, he had smelled a lion. He had not seen the animal; later he could not be sure if it had ever existed. But the odor of the beast had been unmistakable: a must of urine, fur, and damp. The cows, too, had sensed it. They circled and drew in on themselves. Okiri had clutched more tightly at the thin staff he was carrying. If the animal had come he would have shouted and banged the ground, but he knew within himself that this would do no good, that the lion, if she wanted, would take a calf. The boy knew he was no more a threat to the lion than the cows were, but he was willing to do what was expected of him.

Then, when the child had steeled himself for his gesture, as quickly as the atmosphere of attack had come, it vanished. The air was clear. All that remained was the cattle's irritation: a shrugging of haunches, a jittery stamping of hooves. Okiri was scornful of the cows' vainglory when the danger was passed, but he was proud of himself. He had passed a test of his own devising, without the aid or witness of anyone else. He was no longer afraid of lions.

Twice as he walked, the inspector thought he heard breathing behind him. He would shift in the path and stare among the trees, but there was nothing to be seen, just the even rows of thick-trunked palms standing rigid, silent in the suddenly windless night. The breathing that he heard—perhaps his own—faded back into the boom and hiss of the surf.

He resumed his steps up the slope to the rocky outcrop. The ground was now bare of trees. Although the black mass of the palms behind him provided swatches of camouflage, if eyes were searching for him he would now be visible from the beach. As he reached the rocks, Okiri quickly squatted behind the first boulder.

184

He had risen higher than he thought. The shoreline, fore-shortened from his viewpoint, seemed as distant as a horizon. The grays and dark blues of the shallow sea bottom mixed shadows in the evening light, until a ragged line of seaweed lay at the tidal edge, dotted with glimmering bodies of jellyfish flung by the surf. To the south he could see clearly along the beach until the sand bent around a small promontory a long mile down the coast. But to the north the rocks themselves obscured his view. If Bimji had passed over to that side of the boulders, Okiri would not be able to spot him without revealing his own position.

The detective scanned the wall of rocks that stretched to the giant boulder rearing up at the water's edge. There was no one visible on the open beach. If in his climb up the hill he had passed Bimji, then the Asian must have been still in the trees, hidden somewhere along the edge of the path. Again the inspector heard labored breathing, but this time it was only memory, a sound inside his mind. Before him, silhouettes of seabirds stitched the low moon. Their calls scratched the surf. Below, from beside the immense boulder, Okiri heard a human voice.

CHAPTER XX

"OVER HERE, BIMJI. Away from the water."

Bimji, emerging from the trees, turned to his left. Grimes was leaning against the huge boulder, quiet, almost immobile. The Asian saw him draw on his cigarette, Grimes's left hand lightly bracing his opposite wrist.

"Your arm is better now, Jonathan?"

The American had not thought of his wrist for days. He shook it gingerly. "I guess so, just a twinge." He dropped the cigarette to the sand and pushed it beneath the surface with his shoe.

Bimji squatted on a low rock, rubbing his knees as he sat. "Did you walk from town?"

Grimes frowned. "From town? You mean Malindi? No. Why?"

"There are so many footsteps," the Asian said. He took a penlight from his pocket and cast the thin glow over the beach. Faint lines of steps ran to the boulder and out along the water's edge. The schoolteacher's eyes followed the ray of light.

"I guess I've done a lot of pacing around," he said. His voice surprised him. It was cold and foreign to him, as if it had come from a shorebird and not his own throat.

Bimji pressed the clip of the penlight. The narrow beam vanished. The muscles at the back of his neck were tight. He wanted to sleep.

"You have my money, Jonathan?"

Grimes nodded. He did not look at Bimji. "It's still around my waist," he said. "Believe me, I'd much rather you had it." Lifting the bottom of his shirt, Grimes unlaced the ancient money belt. He folded it and then reached his hand out to the Asian.

As Bimji's fingers closed over his father's purse, the two Africans stepped from behind the giant boulder. Kimathi held an automatic rifle in one arm and a kerosene lamp in the other. He passed the lantern to Grimes who, with difficulty, lit the wick. Pausing for the light to flare, Mathenge approached the stone where the Asian sat. He walked slowly, sauntering, on promenade, his left hand around the lion-headed cane. He took the wallet gently from Bimji's grasp as if he were correcting a greedy infant.

"You know that is not good money, Mr. Bimji. I must see it first. For the government, you know." He opened the wallet and rifled through the bills. Grimes turned away. Mathenge knew what was in the wallet. He had gone through it all before.

"It is black money, isn't it? Else you would not be taking all these elaborate precautions." Mathenge waved his hand airily at the night.

Bimji did not get up. He rubbed a hand through the thin hairs at his temple. He did it slowly, with deference to Kimathi who was standing before him like an agitated terrier. The Asian's fingers, brushing his cheek as he brought them back, released a zephyr of patchouli into the air. Bimji breathed the smell of dead flowers. He looked at the large African.

"I am supposed to be knowing who you are?" he said. The song of his accent made it both question and statement.

"I am Mathenge. The minister. You have heard of me."

"And you of me, apparently." Bimji smiled.

Mathenge stared at him for a moment. "I have heard nothing good."

He looked at the wallet in his hand, then with exaggerated motion dropped it to the sand at Bimji's feet.

"Your friend here"—Mathenge pointed to Grimes—"has told me you killed Isaac Moguru."

Bimji studied Grimes and the small man with the rifle, then lifted his head to the minister. "I was present at his death."

"You did not cause it?"

"He caused it himself. Mr. Moguru was a temperamental man. Jonathan can tell you that. He was trying to blackmail me. The kind is not so uncommon. They have been rejected for a position in a bank, so they teach secondary school. They are ambitious, but they are not successful. They take offense easily."

A sudden breeze twisted around the rocks and the hillside palms bent in the wind, crying with the strain. The four men looked up at the line of boulders at the treetops. Mathenge sat down next to Bimji, resting the dark cane across his thighs.

188

"You knew he worked for me?"

"That was the rumor, but I do not believe all rumors. Otherwise there are so few people one can trust. I suspected he had something to do with your people. But I did not know it until now."

Grimes watched the seated men with heightened care. His senses seemed to sharpen in proportion to his feeling of powerlessness. The two men were large and heavy, dark in the night. They blotted out the light reflected from the beach and sea behind them.

Again Bimji spoke. "I was not challenging you, Mr. Minister. I was tending to my business. Your Moguru had written me a note." Bimji laughed, a ripple of motion down his arms. "It had to be written, of course, because of what our friend Jonathan had done to his jaw. He said he knew that Landers and myself were poachers." The Asian leaned forward, confiding in Mathenge. "This was not a big surprise, you know. Many people knew that— it is merely a business expense. So Landers and I were to meet him at a place we all knew. Jonathan here can describe it to you, I am sure. Tell the minister about it, Jonathan."

Grimes did not want to be drawn into Bimji's speech, but the Asian did not let go.

"Oh, surely you know. The place where Landers and I buried our ivories."

"I don't know what you're talking about, Bimji."

"But you must. You are such a student of our natural history." The Asian sighed and turned again to Mathenge. "When ivory is poached, it must be hidden. Then it becomes red when it is buried and must be very thoroughly cleaned before it can be used by the jewelers. But of course, you know that yourself, Mr. Mathenge."

Kimathi dropped a hand from the rifle stock and slapped Bimji across the face. A trace of blood flowed from near the bone. As he wiped it from his cheek it mixed with the scent of the hair oil still on the Asian's fingertips.

"I wish you Africans would learn to cut your nails. It is so unclean."

Kimathi stepped forward again and was stopped by Mathenge's cane across his stomach. "Let him be!" the minister growled. He handed the Asian the handkerchief from his breast pocket, and the gunman retreated back to the dark side of the boulder.

Bimji wiped the blood and then, with the clean side of the handkerchief, gently patted his brow.

"We would bury our tusks by a large baobab tree, next to the *wadi* that is called the Ulu River, during the rains. It is a very big tree in an area of very small trees. There is no mistaking it. Moguru had discovered what we kept there, and it is there we went to see him." Bimji paused. "Am I going too fast? As this business is official"— Bimji sucked the word as if it were a sweet lozenge— "I thought perhaps you would want someone to take down my statement. Jonathan perhaps, since this other gentleman's hands are busy. Jonathan would make a good clerk."

"There is no need of that, Mr. Bimji. Go on."

"Landers was more upset about Moguru's note than I was. He was used to paying officials. He did not appreciate private citizens interfering in this way." Bimji shook his head slowly in the moonlight. "You see, Mr. Minister, we did not know he was so highly connected.

"Landers had brought his rifle in the back seat of the Land Rover. He drove. I cannot drive. It is one of the little skills of living in this country I have never managed to learn. Moguru was waiting for us at the tree by the Ulu. He had some kind of pistol, which he had kept in the pocket of his jacket. With the jaw, you know, it was not easy to understand him. He could talk a little, but only in a whisper. Sometimes when we could not follow him, he had to write things down. This required him to squat in the light of our headlights. He himself had only a bicycle with a small candle that did not burn in the wind, as it would not burn here. Of course, he could not keep his hand on the pistol when he was writing. All these"—Bimji's eyebrows pursed together for an instant; he blinked, as if smoke had been blown in his face—"these difficulties made it hard for him to be as threatening as he would have liked. You must forgive us, Mr. Mathenge, if we laughed at him."

The Asian rested his palms on his heavy knees. In Grimes's eyes, he seemed to be turning into a statue. "If we had known he spoke for you, Mr. Minister, we would have been kinder. To us, he was just another chit to pay. He told us he knew that we buried illegal ivories at this tree and that Landers led groups that killed the elephants. He said he had photographs. This was meant to be a surprise, but there is only one place to develop photos in Kigeli. That is the shop of my cousin Parmar. The pictures showed a big man in a big hat with a gun. The face was like a bit of squashed rice. I do not think a magistrate would have been impressed."

Bimji stopped a moment to clear his throat. His voice was rising in volume as he spoke, as if he were trying to maintain his dignity by the strength of the sound of his words. Mathenge sat silent with his cane. His dark red eyes focused, now on the Asian's hands, now on his face, measuring him.

"Moguru said to us he would not be content with a single payment. He wanted a more permanent partnership. Landers told him—he was not a man of courtesy—to bugger off. The school-teacher took offense. He began to wave the pistol about. Landers tried to reach for the gun but he could not knock it out of Moguru's hands, so both of them were holding the gun.

"The rifle was still in the back of the Land Rover, but I was not sure how long it would take me to get it. Besides"—again Bimji smiled—"as I have told you, I am not so good with machines. I did not know if I could work a rifle as well as your friend here. But Landers had a knife in the front seat, the kind he used in skinning the animals. It was in a sheath, but the sheath was unbuttoned. I took it." The Asian rubbed the tops of his thighs gently with his hands, as if he were smoothing his trousers. "I used it. Moguru's finger was still on the trigger. As he fell he fired a single shot into the air. It hit only the baobab tree."

Bimji raised his eyes to the American against the rock. There was a buzzing in Grimes's fingers, as if every gesture of Bimji's brought with it a shock of warning. "It was the knife that made me think of you, Jonathan. It was like one I have seen in your kitchen. It is from France or Germany, no doubt. You have so many fine things."

Mathenge eased himself to his feet. He stood with his back to Bimji, staring out at the water, the cane's tip resting in the sand. He spoke to the sea.

"Moguru did not mention my name?"

"He said nothing to me, Mr. Mathenge. He said he had important friends. But in our country, you know, everyone has important friends. I was not daring anyone. I was tending to my business. Jonathan knows that."

Bimji turned suddenly, reaching out. For the first time Grimes sensed real fear in the Asian's voice. "Tell him about me, Jonathan. Vouch for me!"

The minister shifted his weight. "I have no interest in Mr. Grimes's opinion." Mathenge began to walk toward Bimji's stone. The water behind him sparkled around his outline. With each step he grew bigger in Bimji's eyes, his shape blotting out the sea in blackness. When he reached the place where the merchant sat, the

African lifted the lion-headed cane swiftly in the air and smashed it into the skull, once, and then a second time, the sound of an ax felling wood. Bimji made not the slightest move before the blow. He tumbled forward from the stone seat, the stain of dark blood spreading from behind his ear.

With the cane's silver tip, the minister prodded at the Asian's cheekbone, turning the face and the open eyes, up to the starlight. Grimes saw Bimji's lips barely parted as if he were about to speak, his words unformed. Mathenge walked the few steps to the water's edge and, in the sea, washed the sculptured head of the cane clean of blood, as if he were quenching a torch.

"If he is not finished, Kimathi, you will . . ."

"*Ndiyo, bwana.*"

The small man with the rifle in his hands fired a single shot at the base of the Asian's neck.

"And now the other."

Kimathi turned toward Grimes and lifted his rifle. He could not see the man behind him, springing from the rocks. Okiri twisted the rifle from Kimathi's hands, the detective's long arms reaching out and over the smaller man, encircling his head and wrenching it to the ground. The falling Kimathi made what seemed a single, desperate grab for the gun, a spasm of his arms. Okiri swiftly swung the rifle's butt into the little man's jaw.

Mathenge, having run up from the sea as best he could, stood with his weighted cane, ten feet away. For an instant, both men faced each other. Then Mathenge lifted his arm. Okiri saw the staff's tip, a yellow star, catch the flame's light from the spilled lantern at his feet. Mathenge reached in his vest with his free hand, and, without thought, before the motion was complete, Okiri fired. The minister fell, a huge fruit dropping to the beach, a bullet through his heart.

The detective's hands left the gun, and the rifle fell to the ground. Okiri backed up a few paces, as if to run, then froze and released himself. He kicked sand over the tipped lantern until the flame choked to a thin plume of black smoke. He lifted his eyes to the forgotten American before the boulder. Grimes was trembling, his back pressed against the stone, his face white, his arms stretched along the giant rock.

"I am a policeman," Okiri said. He swung his head around and brought his hands to his chest as if to search his pockets for a badge, credentials. Foolish, he let his arms hang loose, a long, ungainly bird. Walking to Mathenge's body, he kneeled to test the pulse at the minister's neck. "This man is a government official." He spoke to himself. Suddenly he grabbed the fallen rifle, stared at it a moment, then placed it on top of the stone where Bimji had sat and ran to the other fallen African.

Grimes spoke as the detective reached down to wipe the blood that shone on Kimathi's lips. "I think you killed him. I think you broke his neck." Grimes brought his hand forward to his forehead. He was astounded by his own fingers. It was the first movement he had made since the shudder that had shaken his body when Mathenge brought the cane down on Bimji's skull.

As Okiri placed one hand underneath Kimathi's neck, the little man's head swung back crazily over the detective's palm. The eyes were blank and open, the pupils wide. Okiri stared at Grimes. Fine lines of sweat crossed his cheeks. He grabbed Grimes's arm, the African's fingers on the healing wrist, wrapping it in pain.

"You did nothing," Okiri said. "Why did you not stop it?"

Grimes took a step away from the detective, a step toward the water. "I tried to."

"I saw nothing."

"I couldn't make myself move."

Grimes looked about him—the smoldering fire at the feet of the three dead men, the rocks, the sea. The two Africans lay stretched on their backs before Okiri. Bimji lay turned in on himself, heavy arms clasping his knees, blood-wet sand coating the disfigured skull.

"They were holding me here against my will. They wanted this man"—Grimes pointed to where Bimji lay huddled—"because he—"

"I heard his speech, *mzungu*." Okiri dropped the American's wrist and paced along the sand. He was trying to contain himself. He felt too strong, as if everything he touched or looked at might be destroyed by that touching, that looking, alone. Again he picked up the rifle and turned around. "You are Grimes?"

"Yes."

"The teacher?"

Grimes nodded.

"I have your picture in the car." Okiri did not know why he said the words. "I mean that I know who you are."

He sat on the rock. He was leaning far over as if there were a pain in his belly. He stretched his hand through the sand, to calm himself. The sand was dry, running through his fingers. It held a trace of the warmth of the day. For an instant he sat in the yard of his home: an afternoon, a wooden chair on the grass, sunlight falling on the skin of his arms, bathing the top of his head. From the ground he picked up an orange his aunt had given him. He closed his eyes. The sunlight smoothed his eyelids.

"You've killed a powerful man."

Grimes moved slowly, tentatively, toward the seated African. He opened his arms as he walked as if to show Okiri he had no weapon. The detective straightened himself in his seat. Behind him the wind surged, and the palms cried again as they had when Mathenge and Kimathi had questioned Bimji. But beneath the sound of the wind was now a new vibration, a low pulsing echo off the rocks.

The policeman's voice was low and steady. "I know that. He had killed others. He would have killed you." A composure was settling over Okiri. He sat erect. His hands no longer trembled.

Grimes stopped where he stood. The African looked beyond him. The noise of the motor surrounded them now as the launch from Bimji's brother's boat approached the shore. The two men saw first the twin lanterns on the prow and then the shape of the low, long boat cutting the waves, turning a wake of bright, moonlit foam.

Okiri lifted the rifle as the boat neared. Cautiously, Grimes placed his hand on the barrel.

"They're not from Mathenge. They're friends."

He hoped they were friends. Except for Ellen, whose face he could see with a telescopic intensity, Grimes did not know who was in the boat. He could make out two other figures near the small outboard motor at the back of the launch. But he feared the uncertainty of the stranger who had saved his life more than whoever might have been sent from the dhow. As the boat skidded close to the shore, Grimes ran down to meet it, splashing knee-deep in the warm surf. He stretched his arms to the wooden rail and pulled Ellen's hand toward him.

"Bimji's dead. Don't let his brother see him."

"His brother's not here."

Grimes heard the motor shut down, and Ellen nodded back toward the stern. A sailor with broad features and a massive, shaved head was tossing a line to a long-limbed Arab boy.

On the beach, the inspector had already recognized the captain from the Mombasa harbor. As Grimes whispered to Ellen what had happened, Okiri called to the sailor in a last, official voice. "The man you are to meet is dead. I am from the police."

Grimes turned back inland at the words, leaving Ellen. He ran to Okiri.

"Officer . . ."

"My name is Okiri. Call me by my name."

"You've got to—"

Okiri's dark eyes looked straight at Grimes's own. "You should not have involved yourself"—he looked to Ellen wading in the surf—"neither of you. They will be hard with you."

Gently, the American touched the tall man's shoulder, as if to turn him around. Grimes was surprised at his own audacity. He wanted to shake him, to make him see. "You're not going to take us back. You can't." Both his hands were now on Okiri's shoulders, lifted up. "It's not safe. For you. They would just send us out of the country. But they will hang you if you go back. You're an outlaw."

A tremor of doubt ran through Okiri that was followed by a certainty, grave as stone. "An outlaw?"

"You've killed a government minister. They won't listen to explanations, yours or ours."

The inspector's hands clenched around the rifle. He felt as if he were in the water, swimming in the sea behind them, a long way from his home.

"You've got to come with us to the boat. His brother can take us out of the country before anyone finds the bodies."

Okiri shrugged his shoulders away from the schoolteacher's grip, without effort or even attention, as an animal would shake off a fallen leaf. He moved his head slowly in a wide arc from side to side. It was more the smooth and graceful gesture of an old man hearing a sad story than one of denial. But then, as Okiri's large eyes swept the sand, the movement of his head picked up speed and violence. The grace and smoothness were replaced by a savagery. Okiri dropped the rifle and raised his fists above his head in a motion of infinite grief until it looked to Grimes as if the African were struggling with a spirit, trying to shake off, to drive away, a deep and toxic sting.

When, as suddenly as it had come, the spasm ended, Okiri was still. His face was emptied of fierceness, but his voice smoldered. "Go home," he said. "By yourselves. These are not your quarrels."

Grimes stepped back in the sand. He made a sign to Ellen, who stopped where she stood near the dark water. By Bimji's curled and fallen body, the dhow captain and the boy kneeled in the sand. They tugged at the Asian's heavy limbs—the captain at Bimji's head, the boy at his feet—until the body lay straight and decorous. The *nakhoda* closed the dead man's eyes. With care they lifted him and, walking to the water's edge, laid him in a sling of canvas the boy had brought from the launch.

The body was brought over the side, the sailors' feet sinking into the soft sand underneath the weight. Then the captain climbed over and rested Bimji in the dark bottom. He moved back to the small motor and busied himself with the engine, waiting. Grimes scrambled up the sand toward Okiri.

"Jonathan!" Ellen cried. "Let him be. You've done what you can."

But Grimes continued up the beach. It was he who had failed the policeman, he told himself, he who had brought it all upon this stranger. He called one last time, "You've got to come with us."

Okiri picked up the fallen rifle and turned to face the schoolteacher. "You will leave now," he said. "I am not like you. I am home."

Grimes let Ellen lead him back to the water, his face pale in the moonlight, his hand trembling in her own. When they reached the boat the *nakhoda* gunned the motor, and the boy, still waist deep in the surf, pushed the bow out into the open water, then scrambled over the side, his legs kicking the air. Once on the boat the four made a silent ring of space around the dead man. None looked at another. Only the dhow captain raised his eyes, steering ahead, straight to the dark ship.

Okiri watched the beacon vanish out to sea. His fear, his bewilderment had left him utterly. The weight of what had happened did no more than confirm the isolation growing around him. The two bodies before him seemed empty. He knew that if he put his ear to the dead men's breasts he would hear only wind. He did not touch them.

I am not presentable, he thought. He leaned over to brush the sand from his cuffs, to shake the beach loose from the crease of his trousers, then stopped, dismayed. The fastidious reflex embarrassed him. He lifted his hand, then held it in suspension, as a cloud shift of moonlight lit the circle of beach at his feet and caught the buckle of the Asian's wallet, half-buried in the sand.

Okiri bent to the ground to gather the money. He pressed the

196

wads of bills, thick as office reports, between his fingertips as if he were testing the quality of earth, then replaced them in the wallet and stood erect again. He wrapped the ancient ribbon around the leather and put the money in the pocket close to his breast. With the rifle tucked underneath his arm, Okiri buttoned his jacket and headed inland.